Alfred J. Cotton

Cotton's Sketch-Book

Auto-biographical sketches of the life, labors, and extensive home travels of Rev. A.

J. Cotton. In short, convenient chapters. Vol. 2

Alfred J. Cotton

Cotton's Sketch-Book
Auto-biographical sketches of the life, labors, and extensive home travels of Rev. A. J. Cotton.
In short, convenient chapters. Vol. 2

ISBN/EAN: 9783337212582

Printed in Europe, USA, Canada, Australia, Japan

Cover: Foto ©Raphael Reischuk / pixelio.de

More available books at **www.hansebooks.com**

COTTON'S
SKETCH-BOOK.

AUTO-BIOGRAPHICAL SKETCHES

OF THE

Life, Labors, and Extensive Home Travels

OF

REV. A. J. COTTON,

*An Early Pioneer in the Wilds of the once 'Far West,' Local Elder
of the M. E. Church, Attorney and Counselor at Law, Ex-Judge
of the Civil, Criminal, and Probate Courts of Dearborn
County, Indiana, Ex-Editor, Assistant Marshal of
the United States, Author of 'COTTON'S KEEP-
SAKE,'and several unpublished Manuscript Works, etc., etc.*

IN SHORT, CONVENIENT CHAPTERS.

APOTHEGMS.

' Books are embalmed minds.'—*Benj. Franklin.*
' Good books are the best household treasure.'—*Thos. Dick.*
' The author of a good book is a benefactor of his race.'—*Dr. Adam Clark.*
' A word fitly spoken, how good it is.'—*Solomon.*

Designed for SABBATH SCHOOLS, and for the guidance of poor, obscure
little boys and young men, who, like the author, are destined to ' work their
way ' to usefulness and honest fame, single-handed and alone.
' WHAT MAN HAS DONE MAN CAN DO.'

Price $1.00, $1.25, $1.50, according to Binding.

PORTLAND:
PRINTED BY B. THURSTON & CO.,
1874.

INTRODUCTION.

My very worthy friend, Rev. James S. Rice, has very kindly written out for me the following for publication in my truth-telling Sketch-Book. If it is *short*, it is also *sweet*, and to the point most clearly, *multum in parvo*, as a Latinist would say:

'I, the undersigned, having read a portion of the Manuscript of Rev. Judge Cotton's forthcoming pretty Sketch-Book, and from a long and intimate acquaintance with its Author, feel perfectly safe and take great pleasure in saying that I have full confidence that it will be a very readable and useful Book, well worthy of a liberal patronage and a wide-spread circulation, which I doubt not will be accorded to it. All the little boys and young men of the county at least should be sure to obtain a copy of it. It cannot fail to " serve and please" both old and young, male and female.

'Judge Cotton is " a live man," well posted and up with the times. He has often filled my pulpit, and his sermons have uniformly been very acceptable and profitable to *me* and to the congregations of my people. And I most heartily wish him great success in his worthy enterprise.

The report of his late most magnificent and romantic Wedding Party, which is to enliven the columns of his Sketch-Book, is literally true to the very letter. I have attended many Weddings, but never one half equal to it for number or splendor, etc.

JAMES S. RICE,

Minister of the M. E. Church, and member of the Maine Conference.

NORTH POWNAL, Sept. 25, 1873.'

N. B.—Five officiating Ministers, 500 guests, and a splendid choir, is rather extra, is it not?

PREFACE.

Preface, indeed! do you say—who cares for the preface? Introduce us at once to your little book.

Not quite so fast, my dear young readers. If you were about to erect a permanent edifice, would you not in the first place prepare a good substantial foundation for it? Well, then, what a foundation is to a building is the Preface to a book, don't you see it? No one of you would say to your Minister, don't delay and bother us with your text, let us have the sermon at once and be done with it; you would not say that, would you? True, the minister might say just as many pretty things without naming his text as with it. But it would profit you little; there would be neither point nor connection in it; it would be simply unmeaning, like one 'beating the air.' But when he gives out his text you have his theme, and with it a *point* of attraction, and know just how and where to apply everything as you pass along, don't you? The Preface is my text for my little 'Sketch-Book.' Here, then, we'll take an even start together, now that you have my starting point and the theme of my pen.

Paul's Gospel theme to the Gentiles was simply 'Christ and him crucified.'

My theme is, 'A cheering word and a helping hand,' to all those who need it. Not a fancy sketch merely, but a record of experience, and that by the very hardest struggle of personal effort and continued application in the right direction. Having in the kind Providence of God ' worked my way' from the very deepest and darkest obscurity to a somewhat elevated and honorable distinction among men, I know the entire route—know it all by heart. And feeling as I do that sketches of my humble life and wonderful history cannot be otherwise than profitably interesting and instructive to all who aspire to lives of usefulness and 'honest fame,' I sit me down to tell them just how those high and honorable ends are to be attained. In common parlance, my Sketch-Book contains it all ' in a nut-shell.'

If Paul was less than the least of all the apostles, his record and history are worth more than all of them put together, including Peter, James, and John. Read the first chapter only of my little book, and see if ever a writer and author began so far down at the foot of ' the hill of science.' If, then, I am less than the least of all writers, it is even possible that mine shall be one of the. most cheering, interesting, and instructive histories of its ' kind and character ' that the world ever saw; and so far as in me lies, I shall labor diligently to make it truly so, from beginning to end. Paul preached neither to flatter his own vanity nor to win wealth or fame, but to save mankind by winning them to Christ. If he wrote out a most wonderful history, it was to magnify the grace of God as exhibited in his own life and history. Every autobiographer has himself for his theme, and must speak of himself, and should write out as true and as fair a record of himself as he would for any other man. But all his thoughts and his words and his aims should be to benefit

and save others, and to magnify the grace of God vouch-
safed to him. And if I am inspired by any other motives
I do not know the emotions of my own heart.

I have no pique to be avenged, no spleen to gratify.
My conflicts *with*, and my triumphs *over* treason and cor-
ruption in high places, I leave to history, happy and content with the issue. And if like the great apostle Paul,
'I have been in perils among false brethren,' or false patriots, or false officials, or among all combined together,
the Lord has most signally vindicated me, and I am too
happily, too pleasantly situated in life to find a single
word of fault with any living mortal man, and do not intend to write a single line or word that shall pain the
most sensitive ear. And so, if honorable politicians and
statesmen have sold their friends and their party, and
blotted and befouled their own peerless fame and record
in that 'money-grab' affair, they have the worst of it—
have sold themselves dog-cheap, that's all. $5,000,
$25,000, nor even $25,000,000 would have been no bid for
me. But if they are content I will not complain. God
reigns and all is safe.

But when, oh when, will men learn that ' A good name
is better than great riches?' Echo, with its wonted im-
pertinence, answers back—when?

In this book-making age, various are the causes and the
motives which induce men to turn authors. Ambition,
revenge, wealth, fame, and *vanity* have furnished the
main promptings. Of course, all who ' know me like a
book' will at once and forever acquit me of all the *vanity*
motives. O, oh! But by a great and herculean effort I
have on this occasion so far mastered myself as to say
what is really *true*, that it would gratify me exceeding

1*

much to leave behind me when 'The curtain of life falls,'
—a memento that I had once lived—something to be remembered by—something to speak for me in behalf of
benevolence and truth, of virtue and religion, that in after
times it may be said of *me*, as of one of old, 'He being
dead, yet speaketh.'

Necessity is of minor consideration with me just at this
particular period in my eventful history. In the kind
Providence of God mine has been a wonderful history indeed, and the clear indications of that same kind Providence are that I should write it out for preservation; and
for the guidance and encouragement of the little boys and
young men who are to succeed me in 'The Grand Drama
of Human Life.'

These indications are clear and satisfactory to me—

First, because I am in comfortable good health and
have nothing else to do; no ministerial field to occupy or
labors to perform.

Secondly, because I have one of the most quiet, convenient, spacious, well-furnished, well-lighted apartments
to commit my thoughts to paper that any writer ever had,
or need to have.

Thirdly and lastly, a wonderful Providence has opened
up the way and furnished the means for its publication,
without one single word or effort upon my part in that
direction; and does not all this indicate and mean something? As the voice of many waters, the voice of many
indications says unto me, *write*, and write I must and
write I will for the glory of God and for the good of my
race, AMEN.

As my readers follow me they will very readily perceive
that Nature put 'a pretty good sprinkle' of spice and

mirthfulness into my composition. But what of that? The great Dr. Hall says in his celebrated Maxim Book, that a *hearty* laugh is known the world over to be a health promoter, elevating the spirits and accelerating the blood circulation. Laughter ennobles, banishes gloom, and the heart that can laugh outright will never be guilty of ' treason, stratagems, or spoils.' Laughter is better than physic, and whoever invents a new source of its supply deserves the name of a public benefactor, and whoever can write an article or a book the most laughter-promoting, and at the same time preserve its moral purity, is worthy of our lasting gratitude, etc. Taking all of that to myself, kind reader, I now forthwith intoduce you to my pretty little amusing, truth-telling SKETCH-BOOK.

THE AUTHOR.

CHAPTER I.

It has been very beautifully and truthfully said, that 'the love of country' is a sentiment natural to man and common to the inhabitants on every part of the globe. And with a Yankee, this feeling, I believe, has the strong power of an abiding passion. It must, however, be admitted that 'Yankee' is not always a passport to honor or favor; and yet who ever saw a son of New England ashamed of his birth-place, his State, or his Country? From every place under the arched canopy of heaven, where duty, business, pleasure, or fortune may have placed him, he turns his thoughts and his affections to 'the home of his youth and the land of his birth.' As the *sweetest* dear spot on this beautiful earth, and with an affection which distance cannot diminish, nor time obliterate to him, 'New England' (and even glorious Old Maine), is a land of surpassing loveliness and beauty. If her snows are *cold* they are *clean*, and can be turned to good account, both for business or pleasure. If her skies are not deemed as bright as 'the sunny South,' in the grandeur of her lofty mountain summits, the stateliness of her towering, lofty forest

pines, her beautiful bays and islands, he finds enough
to make his early home exquisitely beautiful and
lovely, and dear to his heart. If her 'cloud-capped
mountains' are bleak and bare, her placid lakes and
ponds, her rivers and her brooks are swarming with
the finest of all 'the finny tribes' known to the epi-
curean world, and are located with enchanting loveliness, and flow through romantic or flowery meads.
Add to all this her proud Institutions of Literature
and Religion claim the warmest affection of his heart,
and the tribute of his tongue. So say writers generally, and so say *I* with all my heart. Good writers
have said that 'Yankee men, nor Yankee principles,
nor Yankee thrift will ever die out while this planet
is inhabited, and should it ever be depopulated by a
conflagration, the last survivor of a smouldering world
would be a Yankee "in at the death" singly and
alone, resolutely trying to put out the fire. And if
it shall ever be destroyed by famine, the very last
loaf of bread will be found in the hands of a Yankee.'
Well, I claim my birth-place in Yankeedom, away
down East, in glorious old Maine, and of course feel
justly very proud of it. Tradition says that I am a
lineal descendant of Rev. John Cotton, of Plymouth
Colony notoriety. I am the fourth of nine children,
of William and Margaret Cotton, of Pownal, Maine.

And now for a little *spice* and 'good-natured pleas-
antry,' I will just say, to the best of my information

and belief, I was born on a very fair and beautiful Sabbath morning, just about sunrise, April 20th, 1800. And if I recollect distinctly, about the first thing I did after opening my eyes in this beautiful world, I raised a wonderful whimpering out-cry, perhaps *first* to let everybody know that I had 'ariv' at last, and secondly, to try the power and volume of my voice, and the strength and soundness of my lungs, which are very important items in starting out in life. My good mamma seemed to think that it required a great deal of ' puffing and blowing ' to satisfy me in this regard, for I kept 'tooting it out' most lustily, almost without cessation, day and night, until I was at least nearly three years old—cried more than all her other children put together, and yet was ' as fat as a pig' all the time, and becoming more so every day. When I was just one month old, I think I was tied up in a handkerchief and suspended to the steel-yards, when it was found that my avoirdupois just balanced 'even up,' fourteen pounds gross. Beat that who can, and I'm sure that I am right in my weight, whether I distinctly recollect or not, 'for mamma said so.' She had searched and searched again, turned me over and searched, stood me up head foremost and feet foremost and crosswise, and searched, if possible to find out what on airth was the matter, ' O what can the matter be,' and gave it up in utter despair, except, perchance, that I must be 'rather weak in the gar-

ret,' not having sense enough to know when I was
well and doing well; and I think she finally concluded that so much nursing would never pay—that I
was hardly worth the raising, and she concluded to
let me have my own way, and bawl it out to my
heart's content.   Well, I ' held on to the even tenor
of my way,' as nearly as I can recollect, until I was
two-and-a-half or three years old, when a crisis 'ariv'
that turned the scale in my favor altogether, and
handsomely.   Now what think you it was, gentle
reader?   Guess again, will you?   Well, I may just
as well tell you first as last, for I am more than sure
that you might keep on guessing until doomsday and
never hit it, *never*.   Well, this was it—for I do seem
to have some vague remembrance of it.   I had *tod-
dled* off into the kitchen, bawling, as usual, and the
tongs having fallen into the fire had become blister-
ing hot.   And now it so happened that somehow,
' by hook or by crook,' I had contrived to get them,
astride my little bare neck, when they forthwith commenced *sizzling* away, and I continued playing my
favorite air of bawl, bawl, bawl.   I kept on after the
old sort, quite undisturbed for a season, when at last
my good mamma thought I had pitched my tune upon
a much higher key, and was *tooting* it out a little
more lustily than usual, and she concluded that she
would just look after me a little, at least once more.
When lo! the hissing tongs were still upon my neck,

and absolutely had raised great blisters. She jerked off the tongs 'upon the double-quick,' gathered me up in her arms and nearly smothered me with her soothing kisses, ejaculating, 'Why you dear, sweet *critter*, you do know when you are hurt, don't you?' Hope sprang up in her heart and she concluded to try and raise me. How well I have justified her newly inspired hopes, and 'what a mighty man' I have turned out to be the record will show most clearly. Whew!

Now little boys, is not that a pretty low starting point, a rather small pattern to make an Elder, a Judge, a Poet, and an Author? You were never *green* enough to place a pair of hot tongs across your neck, were you? And you have that much start 'ahead of me,' in a career of usefulness and honest fame. Will you improve it?—*will you?*

After I had grown up to be a man in the world, and to become 'a man among men,' my dear, sainted mother often repeated to me the 'bawling' portion of my life's eventful history. And how she would laugh outright at my witticism when I would tell her that I supposed when I was so fat and sleek I felt so happy and content that I wanted to 'laugh outright' all the time, but didn't know how. But the tongs sat me right—after which, I laughed more than any other man I ever knew. I did not merely make up mouths and pucker up my face, but I laughed in good sober earnestness, if such a thing could be. I laughed all over, inside and out, and sometimes laughed until I was perfectly ashamed of myself, and the more I tried *not* to laugh the more I *would* in spite of all my efforts to 'hold up.' 'Laugh and be fat' seems to have been my natural inbred motto.

Well that is spiced enough, ain't it boys? Perhaps too much—by far.

My object, however, has been to cheer parents in their nursery cares who may chance to have rather forbidding or hopeless children. For 'behold what a great fire a little matter kindleth,' and so behold what a great and good man a little boy will make— sometimes. And then I would 'spice' my pages a little, as I go along, to make them the more reada- ble, enlivening, and interesting—that's all.

CHAPTER II.

When I could not have been more than about five years old, I gave evidence of having at least a little *think* about me, any how. And that little exhibition was very cheery to the heart of my dear, now sainted mother, who early taught me to say my little prayers, and to commit to memory the Westminster Catechism. The question was: Who made you? Answer—God. Mamma who made God, inquired I. What followed has enabled me to remember it most distinctly. For instead of hushing my inquiring spirit, she very kindly and patiently undertook to enlighten me upon the subject, just as a parent should. Nobody made God; he is not a man, but a Spirit. Though you cannot see him, he sees you and hears all you say. You must, then, be a good boy, and use no naughty or wicked words, for God loves all good little children. He made the sun, moon, and stars that shine so brightly. He made all the high mountains, and all the trees, the little brooks, and the pretty birds; and you must never hurt any of them. And wantonly I never have, from that day to this. Neither have I ever uttered a single wicked, blasphemous oath in all my life. These early religious trainings have exercised a saving, holy influence over me, at home and abroad, in all the duties and conflicts of life.

> Yes, mother, thou art dear to me,
>   Thy name how sweet;
> Hope says we soon shall meet again,
>   At the Redeemer's feet.

And my dear, good father took similar pains with me.

There is yet another rather amusing incident in my early history, which I distinctly remember all about, as distinctly as though it were an occurrence of yesterday. And I will record it for the amusement of my little readers. The old folks of course will 'skip it,' one and all together.

When I was about eight or nine years of age, I was mounted on Doll, our good old black mare, with a pillow-case, and sent about three miles to get a few apples. For young as I was I could 'stick to a horse like a monkey.' I got my apples, the lady owner divided them in the pillow-case about even, and threw them across the old mare's neck just before me, and I started home 'the biggest *little* man,' and perhaps the happiest little boy in all Christendom. Now I was always a very tender-hearted little fellow, and when about half-way home it occurred to me that it was not hardly fair to let old Doll carry me and the apples too; so I sung out, *whoa!* 'reined up,' and somehow contrived to swing the pillow-case over my shoulder, and started forward again. The thing did not work right, it bothered me ever-so-much. But then to let the old mare carry me and the apples too was quite out of question with my young and tender heart, and so I held on to them as best I could, and rode up to the door with as much seeming triumph as would a conquering General enter into a surrendered city. Mamma met me at the door, and all smiling, said, ' My son, why have you those apples on your shoulder?' ' Why I thought it too bad to let good old Doll carry me and the apples too, and so I thought I would just bring the apples myself!' ' Hail Columbia!' I never heard the last of that, and have laughed at the remembrance of it a thousand times since. And now you may laugh at it until you cry, as I do while recording it. But it showed a good heart if a poor head, didn't it, boys? And that's the moral of it all. What saith the good Book, ' The merciful man (or boy) is merciful to his beast.' But rather a small pattern, or starting-point, again, ain't it little boys—ain't it?

I will now treat my *little* readers and *big* ones too, to a brace of incidents a little more creditable both to my head and heart, &c.

When I was about ten years old a man by the name of Dodge, a most gluttonous eater, and a most

inveterate and filthy tobacco-chewer, while working
for my dear, sainted father one day, got out of tobacco, and tobacco he must have, quit work, or die.
And so I was sent all over the neighborhood if possible to procure him a quid. And when I returned
empty as I went, he fairly sighed in his spirit, 'O
what shall I do!' Pausing a moment, he drew out
the lining of his vest pocket, which was perfectly saturated and stiff with the amber of his half-chewed
quids—a nasty, sickening, filthy thing, and thrust it
into his mouth as a substitute for the genuine article.
I looked on with sickening disgust, and said to myself right ' there and then,' away out in father's back
field, ' I will never come to that,' and I never have.
It may seem a little more heroic and manly when it
is understood that I had already contracted the habit
of using a *little* occasionally—could *squirt* the juice
quite scientifically, and bade fair to become an efficient and finished performer. Now I ask in all
truthful, sober earnestness, was not that a very wise,
noble, and honorable resolve for a little boy voluntarily to assume and maintain to the advanced age of
more than threescore years and ten? Beside avoid-
ing the inconvenience and filthiness of the practice,
estimating my tobacco bill to have been one cent per
day from that time to this, compounded at ten per
cent, I find that it has not only saved to me hundreds,
but thousands of dollars—yes, thousands. I *could*

but will not tell you how many. Work it out for
yourselves, and see, and wonder, and then resolve as
I did to let the filthy thing alone. Here is where
my money for books comes in. Don't *that* pay?
My perusal of good books has ever furnished me with
rich mental repasts, my extensive travels have supplied me with sight-seeings which I value far above
all price, and all combined have made 'a man of me,'
an honorable, useful, happy man of me, in more ways
than one. And 'what man has done man can do,'
says an old adage. Try it and see for yourselves,
boys, will you—O will you?

My other little story comes off in this style, to wit:
The winter before I should have been fourteen years
old the then coming April, Morse's New Geography
—a most beautiful and splendid book, was introduced
into our school, and I wanted one very much indeed,
but father did not feel hardly able to buy one for me
at that time, nor did he think I really needed it, but
told me if I would be a good boy, study hard, and
learn all I could this winter, he would get one for me
the next winter. That seemed to be a long time to
look ahead and wait, under the disheartening circumstances of 'hopes deferred.' But I submitted to it
with a pretty good grace, I believe, under all the circumstances. Still the new Geography haunted all
my day and night dreams, and it seemed as though I
could not give it up. Now so it was at about mid-

winter, both father and mother went on a visit 'down east,' to be gone about two weeks. Thinks I, now's my time. 'Nothing venture, nothing have." So I went into the woods, chopped me a load of cord-wood, yoked up Old Star and Bright, hauled it out, and the next day loaded it all up good—for I knew just how to—bundled up my hay, and took the other necessary feed and lay it on my load, as I had done before with father, and at about sunset, as usual, hitched on Star and Bright and started off for Portland, a distance of about twenty miles, to be out all night in the cold, and all alone at that—put up at Buckman's tavern, our common stopping place, baited my oxen and treated myself to 'a lunch,' rested about the usual time, hitched up my cattle, and started off again with good heart under the inspiration of that new book; arrived in Portland market early in the morning, called upon a cousin, told him if he would get me one of Morse's New Geographies he might have my whole load of wood, which he 'snapped at quick' (about half of its value). But what cared I for that. Every thing that I then wanted in the world, was just Morse's Geography. I grasped it eagerly, stowed it away carefully, and soon started for home, almost too happy to live; arrived at home in good time, my dear sisters, bless 'em, for they are both alive yet, helped me to put out and feed the oxen, and had a good supper all smoking hot in readiness

for me on the table. I ate hearty, and then laid me
down to sweet repose and happy dreams. In the
morning 'bright and early' I hied me off to school,
and with my new and beautiful, and long-desired
book under my arm, I marched into my seat I reck
on, in the most dignified and self-important manner.
If I did not 'feel my keeping' *then* I never did. My
new book and my wonderful performance excited the
attention of all the school, and my teacher said, 'I
shall not wonder if you come out a great and good
man some of these days.' O! but didn't I stand
high in my old shoes and patched coat that day?

My father and mother were so highly pleased that
they could not help saying 'that was nobly done, but
you paid a little too "dear for your whistle," that
time, as Ben Franklin said. The next time be sure
to "gather up the fragments that nothing be lost,"
and you may make your mark in the world yet, possibly—who knows?' or words to that effect. Ah!
my little readers, you, too, may make your mark in
the world—who knows?

But was not mine a wonderful performance for a
little boy not fourteen years old? Get out a load of
wood and drive a team twenty miles in a cold winter's night, and all alone, for a new book! I am
proud of the feat myself, even to this day, and have
thought it quite too good to be lost, and so I have

2

taken time to write it out for your pleasure and benefit.

A NIGHT WITH A BEAR—*almost.* At the age of a little past fourteen years, I was sent on business 'away down East,' as far as Chesterville, a little west of Farmington, on the Sandy River. My route lay through Monmouth, and where else I do not at this time distinctly remember. Very early in the morning, all full of hope and animation, I started off a-foot and alone. The evening of the second day, at about sunset found me within about eight miles of my journey's end, somewhat wearied and sore footed, but full of ambition. I was resolved to go through that night. The way just before me lay through a dark, pine forest, without an inhabitant for more than three miles, as I well knew, with large ponds on either side of it. With my heart in my mouth I plunged into this dark avenue at early night-fall. A full-orbed moon was shining magnificently fair, and fleecy clouds were afloat in the beautiful heavens overhead, and gentle zephyrs murmuring in the tree-tops. But manning up my courage I dashed on, seeing strange sights, and hearing strange sounds from the forest and the ponds—a little boy all alone, far from home, and in a forest noted for the habitation of white-faced bears, and that, too, in the night-time! Only think of that, will you?

Well, I was making fine progress, and had got

more than half way through this dreary part of the
road, when I was right suddenly 'brought up all
standing' with a great big white-faced bear, *sure
enough*. It rose up just a little ahead of me, close by
the side of the road. I was perfectly transfixed to
the spot, utterly too much affrighted to halloo, and it
would have availed me nothing if I had. With my
hands upraised, and my straining eye-balls nearly
popping out of my head with excitement, out of sight
and hearing of any living human being save him
who heareth and seeth all things—O what a moment!
And now it moves, and I must be moving too, and I
sagely concluded that if I had to run I would run the
right way, and off I started upon 'the double-quick,'
with my eyes riveted upon the object of terror which
had thus arrested my attention. Having gotten a
little past it, I saw it all more clearly. And there it
stood, sure enough, just in the very attitude of—O
dear me—yes, just in the attitude of—of—a great—
big—black—stump! *whew!* The moon shining upon
a small spot of it through the trees accounts for its
white face, and a pine bough waving in the breeze
made it appear to move, and thus all was satisfactorily
explained. And marching right up to the stump
after 'the Rubicon' was passed, and scanning all the
premises carefully I laughed outright for joy, and
actually wept for heart-felt gratitude to God for his kind
preserving care over me—set out afresh on my way,

and completed my journey before bed time. Receiving a hearty greeting, and a good warm supper, I lay me down to rest in soft and peaceful slumbers.

I record this story because it was all *bear* to me at the time, in all truthful soberness, and do so to exhibit one of my very wonderful exploits in my early youth, as being very justly a part and parcel of my life's eventful history.

Now boys, ain't that quite a considerable bear story, after all? I took a good hearty laugh when I got through with it; and now you may have your laugh—for it is truly laughable. I have, however, some real bear and panther stories in reserve for your entertainment by-and-by.

And thus closes this chapter.

CHAPTER III.

My kind and good parents were not members of any church, but sustained and sat under the ministry of the Congregational Church, and were constant attendants at ' the house of God,' as I said in my ' Keepsake,' and from which I shall quote often and freely, as of right I may well do, ' without a why or a wherefore,' may I not? Well, then, if my parents had belonged to fifty churches they could scarcely have raised their children more carefully or tenderly. Vulgar or profane language, cruelty to animals, robbing bird's-nests, or orchards, and the violation of the Holy Sabbath were all strictly forbidden, and religiously enforced.

We were all very early taught the ' Westminster Catechism,' and select portions, and even whole chapters of the Sacred Scriptures—to bow around the maternal and paternal knee, to fold our little hands and use our infant tongues and lips in prayer to God and praises to his holy name. And as I have elsewhere said, this early, pious training has exerted a saving, restraining, and holy influence over me in all my affairs, and in all my extensive journeyings ' to and fro in the earth.' And at an early period in life it all eventuated in my happy conversion to God, and membership in another branch of the Christian Church, demonstrating the truthfulness of that Divine saying, 'Train up a child in the way he should go and when he is old he will not depart from it.' Parents, do you hear that—and will you take heed to it? Will you?

It is a well authenticated historical fact, that most, if not all the truly great and good men who have ever lived to bless the church, the State, and the world, attribute all their greatness, their goodness, and their fame, to the early instruction and training of a pious mother. For instance, the late Hon. John Quincy Adams, 'the old man eloquent,' said: 'All that I ever have been worth being, all that I now am, and all that I ever hope to be, I am indebted, under God, to the pious training of my sainted mother.' And such is my testimony in all true sincerity and love.

My parents were only in comfortable circumstances, so that my opportunities for acquiring an education were limited to the facilities of the common schools for only two or three months in the winter season, and even that only up to the eighteenth year of my age, at which time it will be seen, I emigrated West, soon married, and located myself in the forest. I was always very orderly and studious in school, though not very apt to learn, always secured the ap-

probation of my teachers, loved them all dearly.
And although 'the birch and the ferule' were in
great demand, and in constant use in those days,
neither of them were ever applied to me save once
in all my school-boy days, and that very slightly, and
for a most trivial offense. All that I now know of
grammar, geography, natural philosophy, chemistry,
astronomy, theology, or law (and I might about as
well say arithmetic too), I have acquired by hard
study and close application to my books, unaided by
a teacher, since I was a married man. For particu-
lars, turn to the closing chapter of this pretty little
book.

The decrees of God, foreordination, election, and
reprobation, were the great cardinal doctrines taught
and enforced upon my mind, both at home, at church,
and in my catechism—all of which were ever dark
and hard sayings to me, and rather ' an up-hill business' to believe.

The Methodist denomination, a people everywhere spoken against as being a poor, deluded, fanat-
ical sect, were commanding no inconsiderable notice
about this time, and from what I had heard of their
' full and free salvation' doctrine, I became rather
anxious to hear them ; and before I was fifteen years
old I prevailed upon my parents to let me go over to
Durham and attend their church just once. And I
was so perfectly captivated that I prevailed upon my

parents to let me continue my attendance at pleasure. My mamma said she knew some of them well, and felt quite sure that they were a good people, and that she should interpose no serious objection, although at that time the gulf between Orthodoxy and Methodism was almost impassable. Yet true to prophetic inspiration, the Watchmen on the walls of our Zion are now seeing eye to eye, and standing shoulder to shoulder in Christian fellowship, as laborers together with God, ' in the kingdom and patience of Christ,' just as they should, which argues well for the speedy incoming of the glorious millennial era so long and so ardently prayed for, and so hopefully anticipated, when all shall know the Lord, from the least to the greatest, when his glory shall fill the whole earth, when there shall be one Fold and one Shepherd— one Lord and his name One. Amen, so let it be. Lord hasten in that blessed, happy, golden dispensation, ' and let all the people say amen and amen.'

In the summer and fall of 1815, a great and glorious revival interest was gotten up in Pownal and elsewhere, mainly under the ministerial labors of the late Rev. Daniel Plummer, a local Elder, during which time I became deeply penitent, and was most powerfully and happily converted at the Paine schoolhouse, in the midst of a precious sermon founded upon ' the spirit and the bride say come,' &c., pronounced by Rev. Caleb Fogg, a mighty minister in his day. This happy occurrence took place on the evening of February 13, 1816. The following lines will explain:

O I was so happy I shouted loud and long—

'Jesus all the day long,
Was my joy and my song.'

And I went home rejoicing and told my parents and friends what great things Jesus had done for me, took up family prayers, went abroad and prayed with the sick, and stood up to exhort on all proper occasions, feeling, deeply feeling, from that very hour, that 'a dispensation of the Gospel was committed to my hands, and that " woe was me if I preached not the Gospel.'"

Yes, I felt all over and within, that God had a great and special work for me to do, and that he would open up the way for me to do it in his own good time, as he verily did most clearly, which see elsewhere as you pass along.

LINES EXPERIMENTAL,

' Ground out' shortly after my happy conversion, at the age of only sixteen—my very first poetical effusion. Well here it is:

Come all my friends by land or sea,
And I'll tell you what's done for me;
I'll tell you how the Lord did say,
Come follow me without delay.

2*

The Lord did by his spirit call,
His invitations are to all;
    His servants too* did woo and plead,
    That I should to my ways take heed.

If you do not now this good day,
The Lord may cast your soul away,
    Into that dreadful fiery hell,
    With all the nations that rebel.

Awakening thoughts appeared to me
In every object I did see;
    And oft I heaved the deep felt sigh,
    And felt that my poor soul must die.

Ingratitude—my grievous sin
Protecting care had 'round me been;
    Mercy on mercies I'd received,
    Yet the good spirit often grieved.

'Though very moral and well trained,
To sinful pleasures I seemed chained;
    With God my heart was ill at ease,
    A thought enough the blood to freeze.

Then I did read with great delight,
The word of God, both day and night;
    Turning it over leaf by leaf,
    To find some word for my relief.

But as I read more guilt I felt,
Mine eyes to tears did often melt;
    Oft I retired for secret prayer—
    Conviction seized me deeper there.

My life I strove hard to reform,
But could not keep my purpose long,
   Ere I's aware I'd sinned again,
   And faster bound in Satan's chain.

I groaned and wept and wept again,
And often thus did I complain;
   ' Wretched!' I cried, at every breath,
   Who shall deliver me from this death.

Thus musing, I to meeting went,
To seek the Lord was fully bent;
   And O! the fountain I did see,
   While Caleb Fogg did preach to me.

From Revelations twenty-two,
He preached to me a doctrine new;
   Text—seventeenth verse, I will just say,
   While Jesus washed my sins away.

Then glory, glory, I did sing,
My soul is happy, bless my king.
   Yes—this I do remember well,
   So now the time I will you tell:

'Twas February—thirteenth day,
Eighteen-sixteen (1816), here let me say
   I drank from free salvation's well,
   My burthen then from off me fell.

'Twas thus I sought, and thus I found,
And feel that now I'm heaven bound,
   And hope beyond this vale of tears,
   To spend unnumbered, happy years.

•Revs. Plummer, Fogg, Sewall, and others.

CHAPTER IV.

In the fall of 1817, several families in and about Durham and Pownal, emigrated to the then far West, and among them was good old Father Noyes and family, the most of whom were class-mates with me. His oldest daughter, Miss Dolly (or Dorothy, as we afterwards called her), was noted for her great piety and amiability. And without any thoughts of marriage, I thought there was nobody like Sister Dolly. And when she was about to leave the place and country forever, it affected me deeply. I thought her too bright a gem and jewel to be lost to me forever without an effort to secure her heart and hand when the proper time should arrive. And with me it seemed to be then or never. And so, young as I was, I made a proper move in the right direction. And we both took the matter into prayerful and deliberate consideration, and after joyfully finding ' the coast clear' I frankly stated that I felt deeply impressed that God had called me to preach the Gospel, and this might be God's method to send me to a strange people. She said such had been her own thoughts and feelings, and that she should never stand in my way, but rather rejoice to aid me every way she could. And she did that faithfully and fully, to the day of her death. Dear, sainted woman. ' How sweet her memory still.'

With suitable and satisfactory apologies for my early move in this matter, I very easily and readily arranged the whole business in a satisfactory manner, both with her parents and mine, which was by the full and hearty consent of all, that I should meet her out West next fall and marry as soon as it might be convenient. Now was not that rather a manly move, and a great undertaking for a lad of seventeen years only? Well it was, indeed it was, and the making of me, too, in more ways than one, as the record will show.

In December, after our friends had gone West, Rev. Joshua Randall, our very popular and efficient traveling or circuit preacher, on his own notion, suggested to my class, that they or it should license me to exhort. O, no, never, said they all, as with the voice of one man. Brother Cotton is a very zealous, pious young man, to be sure, but he has neither mind nor information to warrant such a proceeding. There is where you are mistaken, brethren, said Bro. Randall. I have sounded him all through and through, and I do tell you that he has a very original and superior, undeveloped mind, and his great piety and zeal, and his love of reading will bring him out. Pass him, brethren, on my account, and you'll all be astonished to see what a great and eloquent minister he will make some of these days.

And they did pass me thus. And many of them have told me since, that the prediction of Brother Randall has been amply fulfilled in me. And may I not ask, with great humility to be sure, does not the history of my humble, eventful life abundantly affirm it too? Read it all carefully through, and see—will you?

CHAPTER V.

I pause right here to supply a deficiency which I could not well avoid. I have just stated that I was, at an early day, most powerfully and happily converted, and went on my way rejoicing—

Full of glory and of God.

But I should be untrue to truth, untrue to myself, and untrue to the church and the world not to say, after a season of great rejoicing, 'a change came over the spirit of my dream;' clouds and darkness encompassed me round about, and I was indeed most sorely buffeted and tempted, and indeed had I been deceived, and 'run before I was sent?'

Who could resolve the doubt
That tore my anxious breast?

The next Sabbath was Elder Plummer's preaching day, and with what prayerful solicitude I courted its coming, and in my closet and upon my knees how fervently did I pray that God would make him the instrument of restoring peace and comfort to my torn, benighted, and afflicted soul! I had gotten

myself all ready for church. I entered my closet
yet again praying—O blessed Lord

> Send some message from thy word
> That shall joy and peace afford;

And as if specially directed and inspired of God in
the selection of his text, what should it be but, ' That
which ye have already, hold fast till I come.'—Rev.
ii.–25.

O, how that text just met my case as ' a word in
season.' And how the good Elder did comfort, cheer,
and strengthen the hearts and the faith of young con-
verts and generally the tempted followers of the meek
and lowly Saviour. And God by his spirit applied
it all to my poor heart, so that I was again ' filled
with joy unspeakable and full of glory.' And from
that day to this, I have never once doubted for a
single moment the genuineness of my conversion,
nor that I was specially inspired of God and moved
upon by the Holy Ghost to ' Preach Christ and Him
Crucified—

> To a sin-smitten world.'

Early in the fall of 1818, I secured a passage on
board of a vessel bound to Baltimore, Capt. Samuel
Wood, now lying off in the beautiful Casco Bay—
Falmouth foreside. And having bade my dear good
parents and friends a fond and tearful adieu, I went

on board with a bold and brave heart, Sept. 20th, and was soon under way for my new home and destiny in the wilds of the then Far West,—more to preach the gospel of Christ than to gain either wealth or fame. Yes, I regarded the then state of affairs, and the wonderful undertaking upon my part, as a special opening of Providence to transport myself to a missionary field of labor where my humble ministerial services might be very acceptable and useful as it came out in the end. Although at that time I could not well conceive how such could be the case ; and but for the

'Lo, I am with you always,'

my heart must have failed me and I should have abandoned it at once and forever. But being full of faith and hope and zeal, having put my hands to the gospel plow in good faith and in good sober earnestness, I resolutely resolved that I would neither turn back nor even 'look back.'

And after we had glided out of port into mid-ocean, being comforted with everlasting consolation and good hope through grace, I sat me down and ground out the following little poem, written at sea, at the tender age of eighteen years only, and now place it at your disposal.

A CALL TO THE MINISTRY.

Since first my sins were all forgiven,
And I enjoyed a hope of heaven,
I've wept and prayed that Adam's race
Might taste the joys of pardoning grace.

    I feel I have a special call,
    To woo and warn both great and small,
    To shun those paths that lead to woe,
    I tremble—still the voice says—go.

Go in my name and you shall find
Me always near and always kind,
To aid, direct, protect, defend,
And I will love you to the end.

    Go blow the gospel-trumpet loud,
    Go warn the gay unthinking crowd,
    Go comfort those who are distressed,
    And sympathize with the oppressed.

Nay, even weep with those that weep,
And feast on joy with all ' my sheep;'
This is my duty, well I know,
For still the voice to me says—go.

    Well, loving Master, here I'll say,
    I freely give myself away,
    O make me, Lord, an instrument
    To lead poor sinners to repent.

And ' woe is me ' unless I do,
So all my friends I bid adieu,
And journey to ' a distant clime,'
Whence we may meet no more in time.

Farewell—my parents here below,
My Master calls and I must go;
Farewell—my brothers kind and dear,
For you I've shed many a tear.

Farewell—my loving sisters, too,
A duty now I have to do.
Farewell—my brethren in the Lord,
Love's tie is not a feeble chord.

Farewell—poor mourner in distress,
All heaven is ready you to bless.
Farewell—my friends of every kind,
I'm called to leave you all behind.

Farewell—ye thoughtless, prayerless crew;
O think—what will become of you
When God shall shall set this world on fire,
And make you feel his dreadful ire.

Come,—go with me,—there's grace in store
Enough for all,—and millions more;
With glory's port now in full view,
I say to all, adieu—adieu!

Remember, this was written at sea, at the youthful period of eighteen years only. And how could I, and how can I or anybody else doubt my very early and special call to the work of the ministry, although seemingly so forbidding and incomprehensible. But then, hath not God said, 'my ways are not your ways,' and hath He not chosen the foolish things of this life to confound the mighty; that the power and excellency may appear to be of God and not of man? It is the Lord's doing and marvelous in our eyes. The ministerial part of my record, which I regard as being the best of the wine, I have reserved for the last of the feast.

Well, after a long and tedious journey of nearly three months by land and by sea, I safely arrived at the point of my destination. I cannot tell you how happy I was, nor how cordially I was received and made welcome to my new home in the fertile regions of the West; you must guess at that. At that time I had no thoughts of immediate marriage. But I had not been there long before Elder Plummer, my father in the gospel, who had moved out there the year before, said to me, Brother Alfred, I am going to give you a little piece of advice. We all know how the affair stands with you and sister Dolly (as we then called her). Now I have this to say to you, that any young man that can perform such a praise-worthy feat as you have done, can take care of a wife, and I advise you to marry the very first thing you do. I named the matter to my intended, or the suggestion of Elder Plummer, our beloved minister. I also counseled father and mother Noyes, and all seemed to agree with Brother Plummer. Of course I had no objection, could have none. And so providentially and circumstantially I was married a few months before I was 19 years of age, and shortly after located myself in a little snug log cabin out in the open woods, where snakes and wolves and bears and panthers, in common parlance, were somewhat as thick as fleas or mosquitos, and went to work with a mind and a will to clear me up a farm to sustain me and mine, while I went about doing good. It will be recollected that I went out west with an ex-horter's license in my pocket, and immediately set about my Father's business. I established meetings in the new settlements, and our traveling preachers entered them as preaching-places on the plans of their circuits. I would give anything for one of my early sermons just as they fell from my lips. It would be a great novelty, I reckon. But then it seemed to be me or nobody. My zeal and accredited piety and the necessities of the case seemed to sustain me and keep me in good demand. And to help the thing along, I found myself in good demand as a music-master and common-school teacher in the winter seasons. I did not fairly begin to be qualified for either, but I was thought to be about as good a substitute as they could 'scare up,' and I guess I was; and by close attention and application I managed to keep a little ahead of the times, and finally to work my way to a somewhat honorable distinction among men, as the record will show.

We had great hardships and privations to encounter in our rude, humble, forest home. There ap-

peared to be little or no money in circulation, and as
a consequence, both labor and produce were marked
at very low figures. Our roads were at times almost
impassable, our nearest reliable mill fifteen or twenty
miles away ; and we had to use hand mills of our
own ; and as to tea and coffee we at first well-nigh
had to dispense with altogether. We did not anticipate much, and were happy and content for the present, looking forward with hope for better times soon.
And our fondest hopes were more than realized.
The forests furnished us with a plenty of fine nuts
to crack on rainy days and in long evenings. Deer
and turkeys were very plenty, very good, and very
easily taken, so that even a forest life had its charms
as well as its privations and hardships. Deer would
resort to their licks, where they fell an easy prey to
the hunter's unerring rifle. Turkeys were also taken
with rifles, but most successfully in turkey-pens
which were built up of little poles like 'a cob house,'
a little ditch or ravine passing under one side of it
coming up in the middle of the pen, poles laid over
the ditch on the inside of the pen, so that when the
turkeys wished to get out, instead of going to the
center of the pen where they came in, they would
keep walking around and around to get out, and so
were taken in vast numbers, which helped along
amazingly, besides the sport of the thing which was
quite amusing.

A few more thrilling incidents in my early forest life will right here engross my pen for the pleasing entertainment and information of my readers. Poisonous snakes were very plenty and dangerous. The copper-head was a *mean* snake. He would lie in a coil somewhere or somehow concealed from view, and if you chanced to pass along in striking distance of him you were quite sure to be bitten by him without any note of warning whatever. The rattle-snake was more honorable. He'd shake his rattle and give you time to get out of his reach before he would bite or rather strike you. On rising in the morning you would sometimes find a copper-head coiled up in the corner of your room, and soon after another one and so on. Mrs. Cotton, one time, in stepping out doors, jerked a copper-head out of his coil by his fangs in the skirt of her dress. I once put my bare foot down close to a rattle-snake as big as my arm. He notified me of my danger, and I escaped 'as by the skin of my teeth.' 'Pretty snaky,' was it not?

Wolves were also quite plenty. They never really beset me, although they were often prowling all about my cabin home and killed all my sheep in a single night in early times. They are not dangerous 'single-handed and alone,' but fearful in a gang. A dozen of them once beset a single man who backed up to a large tree and defended himself with a large club or shelalah, killed about half of them, and the balance took to flight and left him to take care of himself which he did most heroically and handsomely. Didn't he, boys?

Bears were also quite numerous and hard upon your calves and pigs. One fairly beset me in the night time, stopped me and my horse for a season, and then went on his way down the creek, and I went on my way home, 'more scared than hurt.'

Old Aunt Betsey Garretson in early times, went out to drive up the cows, when a big bear beset her. Jowler seemed to say you shall not hurt my mistress while I'm about, and so he nabbed the bear by the ham-string, and then they took it tussle about. Old Bruin (as we call the bear) kept turning round and round trying to get his behind before him so that he could get at Jowler, but somehow could not make that game work; two could work at that about as well as one, and Jowler understanding that game full quite as well as Bruin did. Meantime, Aunt Betsey, with a big club, walked into Bruin right and left, 'like a thousand of brick' (as the saying is), and when she could hit Bruin without danger to Jowler, let him have it right and left with a will. At last, with a double-handed over-lick *ker whack*, she took him across his how do'do department, stove in his forecasle, when he fell quivering at her feet, and she 'gave him Jesse' to her heart's content, 'left him alone in his glory'—drove up the cows—reported progress—and asked leave to sit again. Now ain't that a bear story for you worth telling? I knew Aunt Betsey well, and know this story to be substantially true. Well, that must do for bear stories.

3

CHAPTER VI.

Shortly after, I was married, according to the Good Book; for I most emphatically 'left father and mother' (dear and revered names), and clove unto her to whom I was affianced; reared me a cabin, and settled in the woods. All was one vast unbroken wilderness around me, save here and there a little cabin and a small opening, the labor of the new-comers the previous year. These were scattered about on what was then called Green Brier, as before observed; so called by hunters, because of the prevalence of a brier of that color that abounded in the forest. My cabin was far removed from any other habitation, 'solitary and alone,' at first. I had bushed out a wagon-track, as we call it, and had, also, 'blazed' a foot-path, a 'nearer cut' to the settlement. My mind reverts with an indescribable emotion to that period of my life. Many is the time and oft that I have entered this dismal and solitary homeward path, when, for a good part of the way, it was so dark that I could not see my hand to save me—was compelled to feel out the path with my feet; with my heart in my mouth, my hair well-nigh erect, and my blood nearly curdled in my veins, for the prowling wolves were about my path, and had often raised their hideous yells in my very door-yard. Indian habitations and tragedies, fresh upon the mind, in this dark solitude, and lost in these dark meditations, when all of a sudden off would bound something with an unfamiliar tread, and then a hideous yell of wah-wah-wah-wah, ho-ho-ho-ho. The shock over, you would feel thankful to find your scalp safe, and that the cause of your affright was the bounding of the affrighted deer, and the night-owl, 'in hoarser harmony,' tuning its vesper notes of praise.

Onward you would wend your dubious way, until your ear would catch the unearthly melody of a familiar '*hoo*-hoo,'* which your anxious and lonely wife would, ever and anon, send over the dark forest, to cheer your heart and direct your steps. Reader, this is no fanciful sketch. Often have I heard that welcome sound, compared to which the music of Orpheus and the mellow notes of the Æolian harp would be grating discords. As you came near home, you would see a brisk light, and your wife standing in the door, as if to penetrate the gloom to get a glimpse of you. At your approach, she would fly to meet you at the bars, and greet you with, ' My dear, are you come ? I have been so alarmed for you ; the wolves have been howling back here ever since dark.

---

* *Hoo*-hoo, let the first *hoo* be uttered with a very full and prolonged sound; the other 'hoo' with a soft, sweet cadence, and it will be perfectly musical. Try it.

O! I am so glad that you have arrived safely.' As you enter your neat cabin-home, you find supper has been long waiting; your little boy asleep, whom you kiss again and again; then you give thanks and eat; and after prayers, retire to rest, and after telling many a long yarn, and recounting the mercies of God, you fall asleep in the kind embrace of Morpheus, and your rest is sweet.

Sometimes, as you were going through the woods with a hickory torch, you would frighten all the beasts and birds along your track, and they, in turn, would frighten you. I remember, as though it were yesterday, that when coming home through a by-path, with a torch in my hand, that cast a dark circle all around me amid the green foliage, when all of a sudden I beheld two flaming balls of fire, that looked frightful indeed. What could it be? They moved, they disappeared; with a kind of snort and a bound it passed off, and came upon me in another direction, and then the same blazing balls of fire were staring me full in the face. I tell you reader, it would bring one unaccustomed to a forest life 'all up standing.' Conjecture was baffled, and all I had to do was to trust in God and go ahead. It soon left me, and I passed on to receive another cordial welcome home, with abundant matter of conjecture, and for an hour's chat. It was evidently a deer, as I afterward learned. Hunters sometimes kill them in that way;

it was called ' firing deer ; ' their glaring eyeballs reflect the light in this manner. The hunters took many of them, and wild turkeys in abundance. Well, notwithstanding I was unaccustomed to a forest life, and was often put up to all I knew to get along with the strange sights and sounds that accosted me, yet many a time and often have I left my bed at midnight, and gone far out into the woods to relieve my faithful Jowler, when he would raise the yell, to let me know that he had something treed. If it were on a sapling, I was sure it was only an opossum ; I would fell it, and Jowler was ready for him. If on a large tree, I was sure it was a coon ; would strike up a fire, and wait till morning, when one, two, or three coons were sure to be taken. Jowler never missed fire, though I often shot wide of the mark. Those, after all, were happy days ; and, indeed, there is something so fascinating and romantic in the life of a backwoodsman, that I often sigh for those days again. But I must forbear, and hasten to report a panther story, which *is* a panther story, and no mistake.

A NIGHT WITH A PANTHER.—About the middle of Nov., 1822, I and my lady, with our only child, a little son about two years old, had been to Mrs. C.'s father's, and had tarried until 8 or 9 o'clock in the evening, when we started home, about a mile in the unbroken forest. The moon was shining beautifully,

about an hour and half high—a few fleecy clouds
were floating gracefully in the heavens—the moanings of the night-winds as they gently murmured
through the tall tree-tops, the rustling of the sere
and falling leaves, the shadowing of the silver queen
of night as she was gently sinking to rest, and the
deep solitude that surrounded us, cast a kind of pleasing melancholy around our homeward path.   Still
we were happy, and were beguiling the moments
with some agreeable chat, when all of a sudden Mrs.
C. cried out, ' my dear, there's a wolf!'   Just at that
moment my eye caught the object, some four or five
yards to my right, in an old tree-top, covered with
green briers.   I had just passed a large tree that
stood on the edge of the path.   I stepped back in a
moment, and Mrs. C. coming up, we stood behind it
together, and by side glances endeavored to ascertain
what kind of a customer we had.   I discovered some
animal in a crouching position, but the deep shade
that enveloped him, and my own excited feelings
were such that I could arrive at no satisfactory conclusion.   In a moment or two he squatted flat upon
the ground.   I tried to hope that it was Jowler that
had come out to meet us.   Mrs. C. said no ; fearful
to have him approach even if it were him, I ordered
him home again and again ; but it was ' all no go.'
' You are right, my dear,' said I, ' it is not Jowler,
sure enough, and we must do something soon, or the

moon will be down, and we left entirely in the dark. Now do you take *bub* and go ahead, and I will stand here and keep the animal's attention on me, and when you get a good start I will then follow, and if I shall be devoured, better one perish than all. Take good care of yourself and *bub*, and meet me in heaven, for if it is God's will to call me hence, I feel through mercy that I am not altogether disqualified or unwilling to go.

'Do you think that I would leave you here alone to be devoured by wolves? No, never,' said Mrs. C. 'I can never do that; I will stay by you be the result what it may.'

All my remonstrances were vain, and I gave it up. She wished me to throw the animal a bit of fresh meat which we were taking along for breakfast, and then immediately start. I had many objections to this, but told her to start with *bub*, and I would stand between them and harm, and if the animal followed I would throw it to him and we would escape for life. It was a critical moment, but we finally mustered fortitude to start; my eyes nearly popping out of their sockets, being so intensely fixed upon my unwelcome guest. I fancied I saw him move as we set forth, my hair seemed to stand erect; my blood to curdle in my veins, as I almost fancied his fangs upon me. But no! there he lay until we had gained the distance of a rod or more, then turning my eye away, we 'put out in double-quick time' for our lone cottage in the wilderness, some half a mile off. We had not gone far when we heard him trotting on the leaves, taking a cross-cut toward the house.

'It must be Jowler,' said I, 'but let us hasten.' When, however, we arrived at the bars, Jowler came out of his kennel, and bade us welcome home, and happy indeed were we to be there all safe and sound. As we entered Jowler went in with us. We had hardly seated ourselves and were with gratitude talking of our wonderful escape, and nearly smothering our little babe with kisses, not having yet struck up a light, when Jowler began to sniff, and going to the door raised a portentous growl. I suddenly opened the door, when lo! there sat, on the door-step, the cause of our affright, and made a bound to enter. I caught him and Jowler between the door and both went out together. After a short scuffle Jowler played off, and my friend came and sat down again upon the door-step.

The moon had about gone down, and having what we called in those days, a 'stoop' over the door, I could not yet determine what it was, but concluded that I had had enough of him for once—that I would try and give him his walking paper; and having neither axe or rifle at hand, I took the fire-pole, opened the door a little—Mrs. Cotton held it. I thrust out the fire-pole—a small hand-spike—and brought down, full tilt upon his pate, a fair lick that would well-nigh have felled a beef. He tumbled over, without the least outcry, not even thanking me for my *striking* attachment; picked himself up in a moment, and bounded over the fence like a dart, and Jowler after him, but he soon returned without treeing him, or coming in contact with him.

What it was, I could not contrive. I was now satisfied that it was no wolf, and a panther had not once entered my imagination, and well that it had not. After returning thanksgiving and praise to our unseen but kind deliverer, we went to rest, and our slumbers were sweet as our rude home was lovely and pleasant. In the morning, I went to an old woodsman residing some distance off, to report the case and ask for information.

'Why,' he said, 'it was a panther. He had scented your fresh meat, and had waylaid your path. He was just in the act of bounding upon you when you discovered him. Your timely discovery and the tree baffled him. He intended to have waylaid you again, and would have done it if you had given him time. No light being in the house, he was intent to follow. There are panthers about—I have heard them. It is a wonderful escape that you have made, truly.'

And then I recollected all the panther stories I had ever read, and saw them all verified to the letter,

3*

in the manœuvering of my 'unknown guest.' And at the recognition, my blood chilled again, and I adored the hallowed name of my great deliverer, who, for wise, and great and good purposes, mercifully preserved me, perhaps to proclaim salvation to the sons of men, and to take part in the great and glorious Temperance enterprise; and I trust, in that particular, that I have not been spared in vain.

Be that as it may, I and my good lady still survive. My son, my dear lamented son, died several years ago, leaving his second wife and three children behind him. Two other little sons and our only daughter, and the sweetest one that ever blessed a parent, sleep beside him in the peaceful grave. Our only surviving child is a son, married and settled in Illinois. I incidentally note these things here. Jowler, poor fellow, my faithful, trusty friend, came to a tragical end many long years ago. O, what changes have occurred since that fearful night! The howling wilderness has become as the garden of God. Fine farms, and orchards, and mansions, and school-houses, and seminaries, and colleges, and churches, and turnpikes, and canals, and railroads, and telegraphs surround me on every side. (See my Forest Ode.) And I am now writing this sketch within one mile of the spot where I was beset with that panther, which I might have killed, and, no doubt, should, had I not been under the impression that it was old father

Mead's yellow dog that had become lost. In a forest life, 'Love me, love my dog,' is true to the letter. The real panther or his mate was shortly beheld sunning himself in the lofty tree-tops, by one of my neighbors, when, quick as thought, his rifle was at his shoulder, his eye darting along the iron tube of death. The leaden messenger summoned him to surrender forthwith, which was instantly responded to, and he was borne off in triumph, as others had been before him. This one, however, appeared to be 'what the shoemaker threw at his wife,' as we neither saw nor heard anything more about panthers in the neighborhood after that.

Tender and thrilling recollections of the past come rushing back upon me as thus I write, and admonish me that life is short and uncertain—that this earth is not my home, nor would I have it be. And oh! forbid it heaven, that this beautiful world should be any the worse off for my having been in it. But I must forbear, with gratitude to God, and with a thrilling and abiding interest, do I cherish the remembrance of

'The night I spent with a panther.'

Reader—my unvarnished and simple story is told —truth, every word truth. And here for the present I take my leave of you, and hasten to my prayers and repose. Good-night, children, and happy dreams to you all.

CHAPTER VII.

It will be remembered that I emigrated West with 'a license to exhort in my pocket,' or better, as 'a licensed exhorter.' And I forthwith set about my Master's business with good heart and in good earnest, although under the most forbidding and discouraging circumstances. I felt that I was very awkward, unlearned, and inexperienced. I felt it all deeply and keenly, and strangers said that I was the next thing to 'just nothing at all,' and never could 'work my way.' But the friends who knew me from my very birth, knew all about my happy conversion and my humble beginning, animated by the wonderful advancement I had made during the year I had tarried behind them, still had hope and held on to me (with a trembling grasp to be sure), and advocated my advancement to ministerial orders. And after 'beating about the bush' for two or three years among the 'pros and cons,' the quarterly-meeting conference, which was held in connection with the never to be forgotten Moore's Hill Camp-meeting, thought it high time to make a final disposition of my case, either for or against me. And so it was arranged that I should preach a test sermon

at the stand Sabbath morning, at sunrise, and the
sainted Thomas Hitt was to follow me, in order to
save the camp-meeting interest if I should fail. As
may well be supposed, I spent a restless, sleepless
night, in mental agony and fervent prayer, and the
language of my heart was, ' Lord, seal up my lips,'
or ' give me great freedom of speech,' as seemeth
best to thee. I turned over Gideon's Fleece, and
turned it over again for a sign from heaven, and I
did receive, or verily thought and felt that I did receive, divine intimations of special aid ; still I went
upon the stand so full of trembling that I could
scarcely maintain my critical position. But I no
sooner began to open my mouth than God began to
fill it with ' words that breathe and thoughts that
burn.' I was no longer my former timorous, stam-
mering self, but quite another man altogether. And
if the Holy Ghost ever inspired a man to preach, it
inspired me on that occasion, and I ' swung clear,'
as we ministers say, and sat down amidst a perfect
tornado of amens, of shouting, and of praise, from
all over the entire encampment, and I too was filled
with shoutings and with ' joy unspeakable and full of
glory.' Hallelujah ! Amen !

Brother Hitt said it was perfectly useless for him
to try to preach after such a perfect shower of salvation, and chose rather to change the programme into
a kind of love feast or praise-meeting, and surely it

proved to be 'none other than the house of God and
the very gate of heaven.' After the services were
concluded, the Presiding Elder, the sainted, eloquent
John Strange, of precious memory, the preachers,
and the brethren generally gathered around me
thick and fast, and extended to me their friendly
hands, their warm greetings, and their words of
good cheer. 'The cloud has parted,' said they, 'the
true light now shineth, and the coast is clear. Go
ahead, Brother Cotton, and the Lord bless and prosper you abundantly.' And I was recommended to
the proper conference for a license to preach, and
passed clear 'without touching bottom or shore,'
and from that day to this I have had an open field
and 'fair sailing.'

I continued meetings about home and elsewhere
nearly every Sabbath, in the new settlements and
new school-houses, and had the unspeakable pleasure
to see the work of the Lord prosper in my hands.
And my services on funeral occasions were in great
and constant demand. I have preached as high as
five funeral sermons in one week; have left my
plough in the furrow, and my scythe in the swath,
and turned out my school again and again to respond
to these pressing calls, happy and content to believe
and know that God, in his good Providence, was
making my humble services both acceptable and
profitable to my fellow-men, at least in a very credi-

ble degree, and which services were for years altogether gratuitous. Money, goods, and presents, for
my first twenty-five years, all told, did not amount
to more than $100.00. Absolutely not more than
$100.00, a sum scarcely sufficient to foot the wear
and tear of my boot and shoe bill in the actual service, to say nothing about the ease and comforts of
home, neglected business, and the wear and tear of
body and mind, which I voluntarily and most cheerfully sacrificed at the shrine of duty, that I might
'make full proof of my ministry and finish my
course with joy.' Choosing rather to be poor and
useful than rich and worthless, Moses-like, because I
had respect to the recompense of reward, both in
this world and the next. Love for Christ and love
for souls was the great moving cause that impelled
me onward and upward in this great work of faith
and love. That's so.

One hundred dollars only for twenty-five years of
constant mental and physical labor! Well, what of
that? Was it because my services were not highly
and duly appreciated? Certainly not, because 'the
Lord bless you, and come again as soon and often as
you can' were generally the parting words of my
hearers and my friends, and from abroad, too, the
Macedonian cry was constantly sounding in my
ears, 'Come over and help us.' Was it because the
people did not love me dearly? Why, no, for they

did love me almost to idolization, as they scarcely ever loved any other man, save the truly beloved Rev. Benjamin Plummer, over whom I threw my hymeneal mantle when the measure of my days and the cup of my pleasures were full. There never was a more universal favorite among all the people, men, women, and children. Rev. A. J. Cotton has not an enemy in the world hardly; scarcely enough, said the people, to save him from the threatened woe. And that was even so until the days of the late fearful rebellion, when the sympathizing portion of them broke away from me like breechy sheep over a fence. Well, then, what was the reason that I did not receive more, do you ask? Simply because there was no money in the country. The people generally in the forests were poor and had hard toiling to get along in opening up their new farms. A thousand times, perhaps, has it been said to me, ' Brother Cotton, we all love you dearly, and should indeed be very glad to help you, but it is just as much as we can do at present to get along ourselves, but we'll not forget you.' Neither did they. When the first clerk for the new township of Manchester was needed, whom should he be but my humble self, and that too by an almost unanimous vote against three honorable competitors. Well, that paid some, and helped me a little in more ways than one. So when an associate judge for the civil and criminal courts of

the county was needed, I swept the platter clean, as
the saying is, with four candidates and two to be
elected. I received 2,210 votes out of 2,500, the
highest majority, all things considered, that any
other living man ever received. And this office I
held for seven long eventful years, which helped me
along vastly, as I said before. Meantime at the instance of my friends, I received the appointment of
assistant marshal of the United States, which was
the fattest office I ever held, and paid well too at
that, so it did. And at the instance of my friends,
and from personal and friendly considerations, Gov.
Whitcomb appointed me sole judge of probate, and
then the question was, who shall fill the office. The
people met in mass, and adjourned with the following announcement, which appeared in the papers of
the county, to wit:

'We have been in agony in this matter, but the
agony is over. Judge Cotton is the man without
any more anxiety or delay. He will sweep all before him like a mighty torrent. We can elect him
if there are a dozen candidates in the field. In conclusion, we would say to the voters of Dearborn, go
to work at once and in earnest, and let your watchword be, Judge Cotton, virtue and victory.'

And so it proved to be in the come-out, for single
handed, against one of the first men in the county,
I swung clear with a majority of nearly 500 votes.

I held the office for the term of five years, which I also found to be very honorable and somewhat profitable, and at the close of the term the bar honored me with the following

BAR MEETING.

On motion of Abram Brower, Esq., the following proceedings of a meeting of the bar of Dearborn Co., Ind., are ordered to be entered on the record, to wit:

At a meeting of the bar, held at the court-house on the 24th day of September, 1852, James T. Brown was called to the chair, and Abram Brower, jr., appointed secretary, when the following Preamble and Resolutions were unanimously adopted.

WHEREAS, the probate court of said county being about to go out of existence, the members of the bar feel it to be their duty to place upon the records of said court a testimonial of their respect for Rev. Judge Cotton, whose services as judge will close with the present term thereof. Therefore,

Resolved, That we have been associated with Judge Cotton in the administration of justice for seven years as associate judge of the civil and criminal courts of this county, and for more than five years as sole judge of the probate court of said county, and that it affords us pleasure to bear testimony to his close attention to judicial business, and to his patient hearing of all cases submitted to him, and his earnest efforts to administer law and justice in the discharge of his various and complicated duties.

Resolved, That we entertain the highest respect for the moral worth of Judge Cotton, and part with him with the kindest and best of feelings.

> JAMES T. BROWN, *Chairman*,

ABRAM BROWER, *Secretary*.

Now is not all this worth something? And here is where the savings of rum and tobacco come in again with telling effect. Don't you see it, boys? And don't it pay, and pay well too? Don't it? Over and above all this, to have worked my way from humble obscurity to a dignified and most honorable position among the learned, great, and eloquent men in the community; to preside over them and to be addressed by them, if your honor please, etc., is a pleasing reflection to me, and should be inspiring to all who honorably aspire to usefulness or fame. Had I been cheered and encouraged in the days of my youthful obscurity as I labor to cheer others, I don't know what a man I should have made. And so also let it be remembered that if I had spent all my spare dimes for 'rum and tobacco,' for pleasure parties, for theaters, for frolic, and for fun, these bright honors and this fair record would never have been mine, to bless my parents and my friends, would it? Now, boys, would it? My dear little reader, I mean you, and I hope you will resolve right here, just now where you sit or stand, yes, just say to yourself, I too will try to make an honorable, useful man of myself just as Judge Cotton and many other poor boys have. Well, now just stick to that, and you will succeed to usefulness and honest fame in some honorable department in life. The Lord bless all the dear little boys and young men is the prayer of my heart and the theme of my pen. 'So mote it be.' And I pass.

CHAPTER VIII.

I fairly tremble for myself when I think how much I have written and how much I yet have to write, complimentary of one so humble and unassuming, lest I should be deemed egotistical and vain. But those intimately acquainted with me will testify that I never 'put on airs' or 'cut swells.' None of the very flattering compliments which have been so profusely accorded to me, and which I have presumed for good reasons to record in my little book, were never intended to represent me as being a second Hargraves, a Professor Harrison, a Bishop Ames, or a Bishop Simpson, or any other one of the master spirits or eloquent ministers of the age; but simply, that from deep poverty and humble obscurity—by dint of application, early piety, and correct habits, I had raised myself up to some honorable distinction among the pulpit orators of the age. And should I, in giving a sketch of my own humble history, through false modesty, do myself the gross injustice to withhold from the record these essential items? More especially as I write my little book more for the direction and encouragement of obscure little boys and young men, than to win fame or fortune by its publication.

An autobiographer must speak of himself, that is his special and avowed theme and subject. And if I would be 'a workman that needeth not to be ashamed' as an author, I must make my little book a readable book—an encouraging book—a telling book—and a *truth*-telling book. And *truth* to myself is quite as important as *truth* about anybody else. A poor young man that could scarcely win a license to exhort, and but for a special interposition of 'the Father of Mercies' and 'the God of all grace,' would never have been licensed to preach at all, having worked his way to such an eminent distinction, and having seen so many of the grand and beautiful sights and sceneries of 'this beautiful green earth.' And having been made the honored instrument in the hands of God, for 'winning souls to Christ.' Should he not tell it, and tell it all freely and fearlessly to the praise of his ministry, and to the glory of God? Yes, to God be all the glory—a humble instrument only be mine. The Lord still crown my efforts with success, and keep me humble while I proceed to speak of the triumphs of grace, as showing in a clear and unmistakable light that 'I have not run in vain nor labored in vain'—

'In the vineyard of the Lord.'

Many long years ago, that beloved and eminently

successful minister of Christ, the Rev. Jeremiah B. Sparks, became my circuit preacher. And at our first love-feast he said, 'I was awakened and converted through the preaching of Brother Cotton here.' O, how that announcement perfectly electrified me! When, and where, said I. Brother Sparks now turning to me, said, 'Brother Cotton, do you recollect the time that you preached at Brother Price's barn, away up in Franklin County many years ago?' 'O yes,' said I, 'and we had a preciously good and refreshing season there.' 'Well,' said he, 'I went to that meeting not an openly profane, but a vain, irreligious young man, and would not come into the barn, but kept strolling about outside at my ease. But when you commenced preaching, I came forward and stood *peaking* in through an open space in the walls, for I had heard much about you, and had a great desire to see and hear you; your manner and your words took fast hold of me, and there I remained to the close of your sermon, and then turned away a deeply awakened—a poor penitent sinner—and in a few weeks I was

'A sinner saved by grace,'

joined the Church—and the conference soon after; and have ever since been preaching Christ and him crucified, as a circuit preacher, and have received into the Church more than five hundred awakened sinners, and happily converted immortal souls.' I wept for gratitude. I trembled with rejoicing at this heart-cheering report. Truly, said I, I have not denied myself in vain—studied in vain—traveled in vain—nor preached in vain; because the blessed Saviour prayed *specially* and fervently for me, yes, even for *me* in his last solemn prayer for his disciples, for said He, ' Neither pray I for these alone, but for them also which shall believe on me through their word.'—John xvii–20. I believed through the word of the sainted Daniel Plummer. Brother Sparks believed through the word of Brother Cotton. Brother Plummer little thought what he had done for the church when he won me into it, nor I what I had achieved by my sermon at Price's barn. Neither did Franklin know the full glory of his achievement when he bottled up the lightnings of heaven. And as little did Columbus know the glory and magnificence of his discovery of the New World. So true it is that ' No man liveth to himself, and no man dieth to himself, for their works do follow them.'

I a star in the crown of Brother Plummer, and Brother Sparks in mine. And so brilliant a star, and scores in his, too, don't that pay? And, boys, but for my early consecration to Christ and his cross, to my books, etc., I never should have done so much good in the world, nor won such bright treasures in heaven. Boys, do you hear that?—and will you strive to profit by it—*will you?*

One more case of my successful ministration, and I pass to the consideration of 'other matters and things.' Many years ago, there was a great dearth in religious and spiritual affairs, on Manchester Circuit, Dearborn Co. Indiana, the place of my long and happy residence. The sainted good Old Father Jones was the preacher in charge; and had toiled night and day, to get up a religious interest, to little purpose. He suggested the expedient of getting up a protracted meeting, to Bro. Plummer, who said a failure would make it still worse; but both agreed to pray over the subject, and decide in the morning. Both reported favorably. Father Jones dreamed that he was surrounded by a large army of hissing snakes, and that he was powerless to kill them, and could not work his way out. At this critical time, said he, brother Cotton came along; and I said O! brother Cotton, help! help! help! And, that with an old Jerusalem blade (as he called it), all bright and glistening, I cut my way to him, slaying right and left, as I came; and he awoke rejoicing at his timely deliverance. Yes, said he! We'll have the protracted meeting. And brother Cotton is the man to open the way. But all these things were withheld from me until long after the meeting had filled its high mission, and adjourned. But so it was, that when I arrived, father Jones said, brother Cotton,

4

you must preach the first sermon, this evening. I asked God for a subject, and for power to handle it. My subject was the great Salvation, and the neglects of it. See Heb. II-3. And if I ever had power with God, in my pulpit efforts, it was then. The theme of Salvation had fully possessed my hands, my tongue, my head and my heart, and I was enabled to speak with great freedom and 'In demonstration of the Spirit and with power.' I had never so preached before, and seldom ever since. I was perfectly astonished at myself, and Father Jones and all present were astonished at me. The ice was broken, the interest of the meeting increased; the house became crowded; and business had stopped in the neighborhood, and all were flocking to the House of God; kneeling at the Altar for prayers and crying aloud for mercy. Old father Johnson said he had stood at the cannon's mouth in the Wars of Napoleon, unmoved, but he could not stand this; and he fell prostrate to the floor, and cried aloud for mercy; slain of the Lord by the sword of the spirit. The good work went on, and 75 joined the church at that meeting. And who but I should put the ball in motion? The Rev. Hayden Hays can tell you all about it. Is not that too good to be lost? And how father Jones loved me from that time, until the day of his death. And God Himself, still more than father Jones. Glory Hallelujah, Amen.

Once on a time, in the eventful past, the eminent Rev. Richard Hargrave, acting presiding Elder, called round and invited me to accompany him to his then pending Camp meeting, in Ripley Co., Indiana. I was assigned a popular hour on Sabbath, for my preach. The Lord stood by me, of a truth. I 'swung clear,' as we say, and we had a glorious good time of it generally, all the way round. It was at the very best period of my ministerial life; and I was at my very best too; and that is saying something for me, upon a small scale. After the services were over, the Hon. Thomas B. Smith, our Representative in Congress, locked arms with me, for a little pleasant promenade; during which time, he said, 'Judge, I am no flatterer of men. I would pay you no fulsome compliment; but I must say, that was a most magnificent and polished sermon. I hardly know when or where, I have been more pleasingly entertained. And I do assure you, judge, that it would have passed No. 1 in the City of Washington.' That was 'spreading it on pretty thick;' but I felt rather humbled, than made vain, by the high compliment; though I appreciated it, far above the price of silver or gold. And let me ask in all meekness and humility, when did ever 'the use of Rum and Tobacco,' win such a high compliment, from so high a source? where! Echo answers where! But the best part is yet to be told. The next year

I attended another Camp meeting, at the same place, with similar success. That was surely good, but not the best part of it yet. I had no sooner appeared at the stand, than a young man, came crowding his way up to me; and grasping my hand warmly, said, I suppose you do not know me; but O judge, I am so glad to see you. Last year, I came to this Camp meeting a vain, wicked young man; and when you rose up to preach, I drew near, and stood up by 'that tree yonder,' having heard so much about you, that my curiosity was greatly excited; but before I was aware, your words had found way to my heart; and I was enchained to the spot, until the close of your sermon; and went away 'a sadder, if not a better, man.' I was deeply convicted; struggled and groaned for Salvation, for several weeks; when God converted my soul and gave me great peace in believing. I immediately joined the Church; and to-day, I am going on my way rejoicing to meet you in heaven. O I am so glad to meet you here again. Now my young readers, which do you suppose afforded me the greatest pleasure—the high and flattering compliment of my highly appreciating friend, Hon. Tho. B. Smith, or the report of this happy convert; through my humble instrumentality; of this poor penitent sinner; a sinner saved by grace. This is not vain glorying; but magnifying that grace which has raised up such a humble instrument to ac-

complish such wonders in the church of God. And
the savings of 'Rum and Tobacco ,' is the key that
unlocks it all. Little boys, you can all see, without
being told ; where the early piety—where the 'Rum
and Tobacco' questions come in. Does it pay? or
rather does it not pay, an hundred fold, even in this
life.

Well, at another Camp meeting, at Moore's Hill,
I preached with great freedom, and apparently with
much acceptibility. And after the services were over,
the late lamented professor Adams and the excellent
Col. J. W. Eggleston, locked arms with me for a
pleasant little promenade, when they very modestly
paid me as high a compliment as did Col. Smith.
And even that eminent divine Dr. F. C. Holliday
shouted aloud in his tent; and greeted me with, why
'judge you fairly towered aloft to-day. '

Now, although I do not intend to encumber my
pages with anything controversial, either politically or
religiously, anything to offend or aggrieve the meanest
personal or political enemy , I have in the world, yet,
that I have many such, is but reasonable to suppose ;
which is rather flattery than otherwise. It shows
that I have been no time-server ; no flatterer ; no
double-minded man ; but, a man of integrity ; a man
of mark. And thus it is written 'Woe be unto you
when all men shall speak well of you. ' One to do
good, must confront both 'Men and Measures. '

CHAPTER IX.

I HAVE shown that although the people in the new country were not able to do much for me at first, they conferred upon me their suffrages from time to time most liberally and most freely, which was far better. And here let me add that, just so soon as I was legally authorized to solemnize marriages, I well nigh monopolized the business for miles and miles around, and 'drove a heavy business,' considering the newness of the county and the sparseness of the settlements, and at my best have married as many as three couples a day, two quite often, five in a week, and thirteen a month; and although the fees at first were very small, it helped me along finely, besides affording me the assurance of general friendship and very innocent and pleasing pastime. Some of the editorials of our journalist were of this sort: 'Judge Cotton is certainly a rare genius, possessing greater versatility of character than is often found in one man. He is a farmer, in a small way, a school teacher, a preacher of the Gospel, a judge, a patriot, a universal poet, and a universal favorite at wedding parties, in which he has a great run, and where he officiates to the entire satisfaction of the young folks,

more especially as he always accompanies the notices
with a pun, or a verse or two of his own composing.
He always had a great passion for scribbling poetry,
and we remember that once upon a time he wrote 'a
sonnet' that would have done credit to Tom Hood,
and all about a lock of Gen. Jackson's hair, which
the old gentleman enclosed to him in a letter from
the Hermitage. He is getting old, yet he writes
poetry with the beauty and elegance of earlier
years. His style is peculiarly his own, and some of
his poetic productions have found their way into the
very first magazines of the country.' There! how
will that do? How much rum and tobacco, how
much idle loafing and pleasure seeking will that pay
for? And in speaking of me as a candidate for the
probate judgeship, he says, 'I know of no one more
capable, honest, or available than Judge Cotton, of
Manchester. The high standing of the judge as an
honest man, good neighbor, and Christian, points
him out as the right man for that high and responsi-
ble office.' Don't that pay for hard study and good
morals?

I devote this chapter to 'hymeneal punning' for
the pleasing and innocent entertainment of the little
girls and young ladies, as well as for the spice of the
thing. Now 'a pun' is a play upon words, that is
to say, when any word has two distinct and separate
applications it is punable, and the application of

them crosswise constitutes a pun, and when skillfully executed are very creditable and very amusing, and sometimes most laughable; and a good, hearty, innocent laugh is enlivening both to the physical and intellectual parts of our mysterious composition, and should rather be fostered and encouraged than rebuked and suppressed. Turn back to my preface, and read over again what Dr. Hall says upon this subject. I have already stated that somehow and for some reason I have had the good fortune to secure a very liberal and extensive patronage, which supplied me with punning materials in great abundance to work up at my leisure for a little agreeable pastime, both for myself and for my young friends, some few of which I propose to record here. And I am quite sure that 'the old folks,' who have not forgotten that they too were once young, will enjoy it quite as well as the best of them. I will now introduce my theme by the quotation of an editorial in one of my old county journals: 'Judge Cotton, of Dearborn Co., Ind., has for many years enjoyed a very liberal hymeneal patronage. The young people flock to him to be joined in one, and he does up the business with a grace and ease that does honor to him. And after it is over he communicates a notice of it to the papers for publication, often appending thereto amusing punnings of his own composition, much to the amusement of the parties. Here

is the one enclosed to us upon the marriage notice
of Wilson Wright and Miss Harriet True.

Discreet and modest from her youth, none surely need
 complain,
Though this fair Miss with all her charms should ne'er be
 True again ;
But why should one complain of this, as all the thought-
 less might?
Do what she may, a privilege rare, she surely will be
 Wright.'

The first pun I ever ' ground out ' was on this occasion, and under these inspiring circumstances. I
had just married a very modest and most beautiful
young lady, a particular friend of mine, and looking
at my fee for the first time upon my arrival home
late in the evening, I found thirty-two pieces of
bright silver money, tastefully enveloped in fine tis-
sue paper, all ' four-pence ha'pennies,' as we called
them. I was much amused at the pretty little fee,
and more at its ingenious and tasteful envelopment.
I presented the fee to my good lady saying, ' I know
that is some of Emeline's work, and I will try and
write out a few pretty lines to accompany the marriage notice before I retire to rest.' And taking
down my slate I soon saw that I had a pretty pun
for the first time in my life, and from that time forward to this day my punnings have been legion, and
 4*

very easily 'ground out.' My next county paper contained this announcement: Married by Rev. A. J. Cotton, Mr. Addison Chandler and the very amiable, interesting, and accomplished Miss Emeline Hedge.

I.

Affection is a tender plant which we should well enclose,
For though most precious in itself, it still has many foes;
True wisdom then this groom has shown, as well I may
　　allege, .
For he has planted round his heart a neat and pretty
　　Hedge.

This received a very pretty editorial puff, the blushing bride appreciated the compliment, and everybody enjoyed a good, hearty laugh over it, and pronounced it a very pretty pun indeed. Thus it was that this punning ball was set in motion, and I have found little or no trouble in keeping it in motion ever since. I thought this little explanation due right here, simple as it may seem to be. 'A fair start is one-half of the game.'

II.

John C. Moore and Ruth Ann Dowden, and others.

　　This fair young bride, full well I know,
　　　　Had goods and cash in store;
　　In great abundance, one would think,
　　　　But still she wanted Moore.

Well more she got, I know that well,
    But still as 'twas before,
She was unhappy all the time
    Unless she could have Moore.

My saucy muse, now I don't choose
    To hear one single word more,
If you don't mind right soon you'll find
    Yourself kicked out of door.

III.

Peter Platter and Sarah McCracken.

Said Cupid unto Miss one day: Ask of me what you will,
And if it be within my power, promptly I'll ' fill the bill.'
That is most generous to be sure, indeed I do not flatter,
Well, all I wish you to bestow is just one single Platter.

IV.

Philip Hunter and Martha Crouch, and others.

Please, Mr. Hymen, say by what rule,
    Was it your own or Gunter's,
You learned these brides so soon to be
    Such nice and pretty Hunters?

V.

Dr. LeRoy and Miss —— Bowers.

Well, well, upon my word, if that don't beat the Jews,
In these ere times, when all are broke, or lightly ' feel
    the screws,'
Thus to be freed from cares and woes by hymen's magic
    powers,
And then so sweetly to enjoy one's own delightful Bowers.

VI.

Hunter and Martin.

This sportsman, oh with what delight,
O'er hills and dales pursued the flight;
How long ' the chase ' I am not sartin,
But this I know, he caught the Martin.

VII.

Peter C. Taylor and Catharine Pardun.

An adage of old is something like this,
' We make our own fortunes,' not so with this Miss,
She trusts all to her Taylor, and be it foul or fair,
As he shall ' cut and make ' she now will have to wear.

VIII.

Ira Tinker and Ella McMullin.

Now, hymen, you have done it sure,
   Else I am no close thinker;
Change so fair a damsel, eh,
   Into a pretty Tinker.

IX.

Peter Platt and Susan Milliken.

Please tell me you that know, those are excused who can't,
How this groom's brother is his uncle, his brother's wife
   his aunt?
Still wilder pranks has hymen played, by the union of
   these twain
The mother of this happy groom is mother to him again.

Try to study it out before you read the following answer.

Josiah Platt a long time ago
Married a fair Miss, I know it is so,
Then old father Platt, oh what a twister,
Soon afterwards married his son's wife's sister;
His other son Peter, not given to loiter,
Soon took for his spouse his step-mother's daughter;
So now, my young friends, I've explained the whole rid-
    dle,
If you can't understand it ' you aint worth a fiddle.'

To understand it after it is explained is one thing; to originate it quite another.

X.

Blackly Shoemake and Mercy Prest.

Thrice happy man, by fortune blest,
Instead of cares, by Mercy Prest;
His days will glide most smoothly by,
Mercy her utmost e'er will try
To wipe the tears from sorrow's eye,
Till he or she are called to die.

XI.

Zephaniah Heustis and Elizabeth Steel.

O Zephaniah! Zephaniah!
  How your poor ma must feel,
To think her dearest son
  Should be inclined to Steel.

XII.

Wm. Whitney of Maine to Miss Jane Fox of Indiana.

Of Wm. Whitney it may well be said that
    He journeyed far from his native State,
      From those deep vales and towering rocks,
    And gave to fortune a successful chase,
     .For lo! he caught a pretty Fox.

XIII.

Moses Cook and Philena Hawk.

    When Cupid bent his bow and sped his dart
    To bring this keen-eyed bird with gushing heart,
    Close by his side friend Moses stood,
    Clapping his hands and shouting good.
    The priest who joined this happy pair
      Has made a world of pleasing talk,
    For he would neither dine nor sup
      Till he had Cook'd this pretty Hawk.

XIV.

John P. Snell and Emeline Flint.

    What a fancy, friend Snell,
      Though beautiful the tint,
    To choose for a bride
      A pretty little Flint.

    Who but thou couldst perceive,
      Without measure or stint,
    Pure love would gush forth
      From the heart of a Flint.

XV.

James McGinnis and Eliza Miracle.

What merry pranks has hymen played
E'er since ' the days of yore;'
He sports with names and Miracles
Till they are so no more.

XVI.

Erasmus D. Hathaway and Eliza Ransom.

This happy, joyous groom was about twenty-nine,
'Mazing near, as you see, the ' old bachelor ' line;
But the blushing, sweet bride gave herself for a Ransom,
And this rescued her friend most handsomely, handsome;
Thus a pleasant affair and the parties well matched,
Judge Cotton, ever ready, soon the business dispatched;
All their friends were well pleased, and each greeted the
      pair
With a very warm blessing and a silent, warm prayer.

XVII.

Dr. C. Pease and Rhoda Conger.

While at the dinner table one of the guests called on me for a pun, when I threw off the following to the admiration of all present.

In this famed world for vegetables,
  There's naught that some can please;
But this fair bride, it will be seen,
  At least is fond of Pease.

You may well be assured that I made my mark that time.

XVIII.

R. D. Brown and Elizabeth Conway.

Of all the bright and gorgeous tints,
In county, city, village, town,
This very neat and pretty bride
Finds nothing like a Brown.

XIX.

John P. Lemon and Kate C. Pink.

My stars! dear me! only think, a Lemon and a Pink
Unite and blend in one,
To meet ' the ills of life ' as husband and as wife,
Way down to rising sun;
Pink is a pretty flower, a Lemon rather sour
Will make a pretty tart,
And give a pleasing zest to sweeten all the rest,
If truly ' one in heart.'
Oh may they each pursue the paths of virtue true,
And ever happy be;
And at the close of life wind up ' this mortal strife '
In love's unbounded sea,
And sail the ocean o'er on that immortal shore
Where all is peace and love;
And with a golden lyre join the triumphant choir
In realms of bliss above.

Beat that who may, and then I'll try my hand
again ' perhaps.'

XX.

Nicholas Echman and Eva Herring.

What freaks of fancy and of taste reveal themselves in
    life,
And often do such things occur in hunting up a wife;
I hope 'twill turn out in the end that Nicholas was uner-
    ring
When he chose him for a bride a pretty little Herring.

XXI.

Francis M. Johnson and Emily Davis. William Jennings and Mary Davis.

' The fair goddess of May,' in her ' floral robes ' clad,
Looked never more lovely, why, all nature seemed glad;
The warm greetings of friends, from hearts most sincere,
Illumed the gay scene and gave it ' good cheer;'
'Twas a season of joy to all who were there,
The viands were plenty and sumptuous the fare;
May the sunshine of plenty attend them through life,
And they ever be strangers to contention and strife,
Is the prayer of the Manchester Bard.   A. J. C.

If that was not a very pleasant affair and a most
delightful season, then am I indeed a poor judge in
such matters. Boys, how think you did I happen to
preside there? How?

XXII.

Thomas Craig and Mary Knapp.   W. C. Knapp
and E. Hults.

> While Cupid strung his unstrung bow
>   To make his arrows snap,
> These brides and grooms, alternately,
>   Just took a pretty Knapp.

CHAPTER X.

HYMENEAL PUNNINGS—CONCLUDED.

That which is worth doing at all, is worth well doing.'

XXIII.

Rev. T. A. Goodwin and Content Craft.

O Cupid ! how thy bewitching melting darts
Unite in one, two pure and loving hearts;
This joyous, happy groom with his fair, sweet, blushing
    bride,
Has just launched forth, on life's uneven tide.
His gallant Craft Content, all beauteous to behold;
More precious far to him, than thrice her weight in gold,
Will make his voyage o'er 'life's tempestuous sea,'
Tranquil and sweet, as 'summer evenings' be.

The Rev. groom, paid me publicly, a very handsome compliment, etc.

XXIV.

Gilbert Platt and Elizabeth C. Wilcox.

Said Miss, to hymen, will you please just change my
    maiden name ?
Your's a fair one now, my nice pretty dame;
That is all true; full well I know that,
But I'd much rather prefer, to be called Mrs. Platt.
The case was made out, and hymen complied,

So far as to change a Miss, to a bride.
When your 'intended' hands Judge Cotton that,
He'll soon change your name, and you all, to Platt.
'Twas done at a word, and a fairer, sweet bride,
You scarcely could find in a whole year's ride.

Boys, what do you say to that—eh ?

XXV.

Joel Bledso and Sarah Jane Swan.

Of all the pretty little birds,
That flit o'er hill or lawn,
This happy groom prefers by far,
A lovely, pretty swan.

XXVI.

James C. Martin and Sue Jolley. Wm. York and Carrie Soule.

FIRST PARTY.

They must have had 'a jolly time,'
Of that, I feel quite sartin;
Since hymen treated the fair bride,
To a superior Martin.

BOTH PARTIES.

These lovely brides and happy grooms,
Richly deserve 'a pun;'
But my muse has tried his best,
And just can't make one;
But may their days glide smoothly on,
And peace, her radiance shed;
And all the paths through which they roam

With pleasing flowers, be spread ;
And may the happy golden dreams
  Of each delighted pair,
Be more than realized in life ,
  And come out bright and fair ;
And many be their days on earth,
  All full of peace and joy;
And may they rest in heaven at last,
  Where all is peace and joy.
And may their parents and their friends,
  Hence evermore rejoice ;
And have good reasons to approve
  This wise and happy choice;
May all their friends who greet them here,
  Greet them in heaven above ;
Where 'cares and conflicts' never come,
  And all is peace and love.

Boys, would you not like to write so too ? Well,
you may try it.

XXVII.

A. J. Cotton and Miss Dolly or Dorothy P. Noyes
and several other Miss Noyeses.

It seems that hymen has his freaks, the same as other
    men,
Just call upon him when well pleased, and he'll oblige you
    then;
These happy grooms, were all 'in time' tired of a single
    life,
They called to see if hymen would just treat them to a
    wife.

Their hearts within them leaped for joy, when hymen
answered yea,
But still I think my dear young friends, there is a better
way.
Of all the ladies on this globe, I'll give you each your
choice;
Bless you; thank you; my good sir; of course I'll take
Miss Noyes;
And fairer brides, you seldom see, than this, or that Miss
Noyes;
And all most heartily approve the wisdom of their
choice.

This you will readily perceive to be my own
happy report.

XXVIII.

Gen. Charles Mills and Eliza Price.

The general fought the battle well, which Cupid first
began;
The fairest conquest he obtained; as fair as e'er was won.
Each 'grand maneuver,' all admit he managed very nice;
And hymen paid him for his skill, the fairest, sweetest
Price.

Gen. Mills was a citizen of Ohio, and I of Ind.
He advised by letter, in good time when the party
was to come off; and charged me not fail him, as
his intended would hardly think herself married, unless I performed the ceremony. Dear judge, fail me
not. I have a $20 bill, in reserve for you, and a
good warm greeting from us all.

Just think of that; a $20 bill, from the highest circles of life in all the State of Ohio. Was that not 'a getting up in life?' And don't that pay for correct habits; and close application to good books—Well, now, don't it?

XXIX.

Old father Hyde and old mother Kidd. His fourth wife, and her third husband.

Now reader, how would you contrive to work that off into a readable pun? A pun is by no means as easily 'ground out' as it reads after it is put into form. Some of my puns have cost me hours and even days, to perfect. But practice makes perfect; and after a while, they come easy to you. But nothing great was ever attained without great labor. The point I am at, is to encourage you to apply yourselves. If your endowments are very small, by proper attention they can be vastly improved. A very small fire, if properly nursed, will soon burst forth into a mighty flame; but without proper materials, it will soon expire. So, small intellectual developments, may come out 'master spirits,' or be extinguished; as they are dealt by. Never had one less mental capital to start off in the world, than I had; correct habits and hard study have done the balance for me. And the same course would have done quite as much for you, in some other direction, perhaps. An intelligent farmer, or mechanic, is just as useful and honorable a man, in his place, as a minister, or a judge. But let every heart and mind be well improved. And now I will inform you how I went to work to 'grind out' this pun. After twisting it about in my mind for some time, vainly contriving to find a fair starting point, I had to suppose that the parties had taken 'a union hunt' as we say out West. No matter who shoots the game, all come in for an equal division of it. Starting off upon this suggestion, it all came into my hand without a seeming effort. The right thinking was the hardest part of it altogether.

And now, for the pun.

> This happy bride and groom,
>   Once took 'a union hunt,'
> How long the chase, I do not know,
>   And say it sure, 'I wont;'
> But this I know, they took choice game,
>   Which they must needs divide;
> But should the groom take this, or that,
>   Or should the pretty bride.
> At last, they mutually agreed,
>   This way it should—did;
> The bride alone should have the HYDE;
>   The groom, should take the KIDD.

All very easy, after you know how ; so is everything else.

The editor of the *Lawrenceville Globe*, Ill., and other Western editors said Tom Hood, Charles Lamb,

Alf. Tennyson, and nobody else, ever beat that. Then indeed have I worked my way up to an even position with the very best poets and printers of **the** age. Ain't that some ?

XXX.

David Porter and Lucinda Baldnage.

' Twas hymen's turn to treat, this time,
As 'a hymeneal sporter; '
What will you have, fair Miss, said he ,
O, just a little PORTER.

XXXI.

John Seely and Clementine B. Cook.

In the parlor, in the kitchen,
Or wherever you may look,
Naught makes home more truly blest,
Than a nice, neat, pretty COOK.

XXXII.

Rev. James S. Rice and Miss——Johnson and others.

This truly happy, blushing bride,
With taste so pure, refined and nice,
Of all the good things in this world,
Prefers a little Northern RICE.

XXXIII.

Rev. A. J. Cotton and Jane M. Hamilton.

Well, well, Mr. Hymen, 'now you have done it,'
Else there is no truth in my little sonnet;
And never shall it be forgotten ;
You've changed my lovely bride, all into COTTON.

5

I have many 'more of the same sort, left, but greatly fear that I have dwelt at too great length, already ; but will venture to treat you to 'a very tall punning snap, ' I once got into, and then I will relieve you, and dismiss the subject. So I will.

Once on a time, in the palmiest days of my matrimonial glory, I was serving as a Grand Juryman in the District Court of the United States, held at Indianapolis, Ind. The Hon. Judge McLane, on the bench. Shortly after my arrival, the Rev. John C. Smith, my former beloved circuit preacher, called to see me, at the court-room ; and extended to me a very kind and pressing invitation to call on him tomorrow, at 5 o 'clock P. M. and take tea with a few select friends. Of course I was on hand all in good time, and in good heart. I found quite a large and respectable company of young and matronly ladies, in attendance. Well, after the salutatory and introductory ceremonies were over, a very sprightly, good-looking, elderly lady, said, Judge Cotton, I am very happy to be introduced to you. I have had so many good hearty laughs at your very amusing Hymeneal Punnings, which I often see in the papers, that I have desired to see you exceedingly much, for many long, by-gone years. That all jingled very finely, and I really felt right good over it ; but in the midst of my pleasant reveries, what should that lady do, but says, now Judge, here is sister Smith, who has

just been married. Can you treat her to one of your
pretty puns? Parrying the onset with excuses to get
time to survey the premises, and measure my distance
and see the outcome, I seemed rather inclined to de-
cline; and ask to be excused. O no Judge; do
please, make us a pun! So said they all; yes, do
Judge! My mind having fully arranged the matter,
I pleasantly said, well ladies, since you all seem to
desire it, I will try and see what I can do. How
will something like this, meet your anticipations?

In this gay world of rich delights, there's much each taste
  to please;
The roaring of the cataract, the waving of the trees;
The wide extended verdant plain, the music of a rill;
But most of all, friend Smith admires a neat and pretty
  HILL.

Looking and pointing most significantly, at 'the
blushing bride.'

Now gentle reader, I do assure you that set me out
'clear as a quill.' The ladies bless 'em, clapped their
hands, waved their handkerchiefs and fairly shouted
aloud for joy. And of course, having so honorably sustained my punning reputation, I was 'lion of the day'
from that out. But the end, was not yet; for in the
morning, before court hour, while I and others were
engaged in a little pleasing chat with Judge McLane,
in came brother Smith; and said, Judge Cotton, my
lady sends her compliments to you, and would be

very much obliged if you would write out that pretty little pun, for her. I thought at first, that she appreciated it; and now, I knew it. O certainly; brother Smith, I will do it with great pleasure. Of course I had to repeat it right there, to the manifest delight of all present; who said 'that was indeed a happy hit.' And while I was congratulating myself with this new triumph, what should brother Smith say, but, Judge, this is Rev. Mr. Berry, our City minister, who has quite recently married too: Can you do anything for Mr. Berry? I involuntarily exclaimed, icebergs! cataracts and whirlpools! what a fix! O, that I had started home early in the morning; but there I was, and must work my way out as best I could. Parleying for time, as before, I saw there was a pun in it, since berry is a fruit. And thus fortune favors the brave. My punning faculties being in a very healthy and vigorous state, at that time, with my hasty forecast 'I rolled up my s'eeves and pitched in,' as the saying is. Gentlemen, I belong to the 'try company' and never say can't. And so here goes, sink or swim. All standing tiptoe, in breathless suspense, for the issue, I began thus :—

Those who are greedy to possess more than their share of
    good,
Endanger all, and fool themselves; just as such people
    should.
But this fair bride it will be seen, is very modest, very;
For she is happy and content with just one single BERRY.

And if that did not 'bring down the house' in the
sense of the phrase, it never was brought down.
But before I had time to congratulate myself, upon
my ready and wonderful performance, one more,
Judge, said brother Smith, and then, 'I will let you
up.' O no, brother Smith; my trusty muse has
played her part well, already; and you must excuse
me. No, not yet. Quite recently, we had rather a
novel wedding in this City; a Mr. Green married
a Miss Margaret Pigg; and if there is any living
man, who can work that up into a pun, you are the
man. Try it, Judge! But does not a time honored
maxim say—'you should never work a free horse to
death.' Never mind that, Judge, let us have just
this one. Hail Columbia! caverns and volcanoes!
what a fix; and what a case. O, that like Alex-
ander Selkirk, I were on some lonely island, in the
middle of the sea; and like him—'monarch of all I
survey, in the moon, or anywhere else. But there
I was, and must make the best of it; and it came out
a double pun, and the very best one of 'the lot;' and
scared up a perfect 'hooraws nest' as the saying is.
Well, I am some at a pun, and know it, and so do
you; and why should I be 'mealy mouthed' about
it? Don't you think, at the World's Fair, as a pun-
ster, that I should take 'the premium against the
universe?' O, oh, 'shame on me;' but here is the
pun, that will speak for itself. So it will.

What various tastes do men display, in the affairs of life;
And odd and many are their freaks, in choosing out a
  wife;
And thus my friend, 'a little GREEN,' as if to run some
  rig,
Chose for his own sweet bosom friend, a pretty, little
  PIGG.

That took me out 'sky high' as the saying is.
Such shouting and stamping, you seldom hear.

Judge McLane said, Judge Cotton, that is truly
rich. If you can do up things in that easy, happy
manner, you ought to be in better business than at-
tending Court, here.

The next morning, he presented me with a note,
from his good lady, inviting me to take tea with her,
that afternoon. And, after the kind reception ceremonies were over, the Judge requested me to entertain his lady, by repeating some of my very superi-
or and most amusing punnings; and his lady seemed
to appreciate them as highly as he did. I fain would
have treated her to a pun; but the name and the
fates, forbade me. I have already said that my
punning fame, cost me great and prolonged mental
study and application. Very well. What says Solomon? 'See'st thou a man diligent in his business?
He shall stand before kings; he shall not stand before mean men.' Prov. xxii: 29. Well, sure
enough; I stood before Judge McLane, of the
Supreme Court of the United States, and decided-

ly one of the very greatest and best men in the government; and that pays well. From the editorial puffs, the blushing smiles of the fair, the general murmur of approval, and the high compliment of Judge McLane combined, which have been accorded to me, I must believe that these punnings possess great and true merit ; affording innocent amusement, a pleasurable and profitable pastime. And that is my apology for devoting so much space to them. Such an exhibition of the kind, the world never saw before. Three dozen, all in a row ; and three off-handed. And that is the good of it. Now think of it as you may, these punnings will give character and notoriety to my little book. Mark that, will you ? And they are really worth more than two prices of my entire work. Aint they—eh ?

And I pass. Good-night girls, and pleasant dreams to you all.

CHAPTER XI.

Let it be neither overlooked or forgotten, that while I have been poetizing and speechifying, and taking an active part in public gatherings and public affairs generally, that I have neither forgotten or neglected the imperative and pressing duties of 'My high calling of God, in Christ Jesus' but at home and abroad, night and day, fair weather and foul, have been at my post, zealously and patiently laboring to 'build up the waste places of Zion' and to cultivate Immanuel's ground, ' now here, now there, at the bid and call of everybody. I have in my time, pronounced as many as five funeral sermons in a single week; and quite a number, in each year. And as I have elsewhere said ' I have often left my clearing,· left my plough in the field, and my scythe in the swath, to respond to these calls of my afflicted and bereaved friends 'without money or price' happy to know that I was operating in the line of my duty; and with the comfortable assurance that my humble services were duly appreciated, and thankfully received. And you should also keep in mind, that I have not undertaken to write out a finished and highly polished literary, scientific or theological work; but a plain, simple and unvarnished record' of experimental truth; to magnify that grace which took me from the very humblest walks of life 'as it did David from his sheep-fold' to be in some sense the leader of his people. In the forest wilds of the then great and growing West, I put on no airs, cut no flourishes and made no swells; yet, I would fain hope, that mine will be a very readable and highly appreciated little offering to all of those for whom it is specially intended to interest and benefit. Let that suffice here.

I now pass, to pay a poetical tribute to Gen. Washington and our Revolutionary mothers, because it comes in place here.

ODE FOR WASHINGTON'S BIRTH-DAY CELEBRATION.

Air—at pleasure.

Come tune your hearts, my countrymen, to celebrate the
    day;
The birth-day of our Washington, with an exulting lay.
In seventeen hundred thirty-two (1732), great Washing-
    ton was born;
A century and fourteen years, this joyous, happy morn.

George Washington—a name most dear, to all the tribes
    of men;
The Muses' theme of every clime, the theme of every
    pen.
Theme of the old and of the young, the lovely and the
    fair;
At home, abroad on seas and isles, aye, truly everywhere.

5*

Our Orator in melting strains, has told us how and why,
We took up arms to vindicate those rights we prized so
    high;
And how in mercy, God raised up our glorious Washing-
    ton;
The wisest, purest Patriot, beneath the shining sun.

He led our feeble armies on, and taught them how to
    fight;
And under God secured our rights, and put our foes to
    flight.

Go back with me to Lexington, go back to Bunker's Hill;
Where gurgling, gushed your Country's blood, in many
    a crimson rill.

O go with me to Bradywine, go back to Trenton, too;
Go read the tokens of God's care, in all your Country
    through!

The gushing blood all warm and free, goes rushing in my
    veins,
As I remember Washington, on Yorktown's smiling
    plains;
There perched our Eagle—bird of heaven, on Liberty's
    fair tree;
And there the British lion roared, America is free.

And in that roar was treasured, all that's truly good or
    great;
The right to worship God in peace, and rule the new-born
    State.
O may we ever worthy prove, and keep unsoiled our
    trust;
And may our children cherish them, when we repose in
    dust!

May bitter strife and bitter words, no more offend our
    ears!
We all are honest hearted men, of the same hopes and
    fears.
This is the land that gave us birth, here we shall live and
    die;
And if one half are deadly foes, kind sirs, please tell me
    why?

A deadly foe, tis true we have, that lures to crime and
    woe;
'Tis from the sparkling poisonous cup, most of our evils
    flow.
It ruins mind, 'O, what a thought,' the nation's sure de-
    fense;
The groggeries, those sinks of woe; O drive ye out from
    hence;
And teach the young to love good books, to love God's
    house and day;
And let their feet be early taught to tread the narrow
    way.

I still think that the masses of our people both
North and South, are sound at heart; but good in-
tentions don't sanctify evil actions. O no! never.

Then God and peace and Washington shall unborn mill-
    ions know;
And the rich blessings we enjoy, to all the nations flow;
Then tune your hearts, my countrymen, let us exulting
    sing,
The hallowed name of Washington, who conquered
George the King .'

The ladies of the Revolution, according to promise, come in here for a passing notice ; and to sweeten the pages of my little book.   Quoting from the production of my own tongue and pen, let me just say for the encouragement of all the little girls and young ladies, aye more, to little boys and young men too, that it is as clear as a blazing sunbeam, in a cloudless sky ; that under God, we are indebted to 'female influence' for this goodly heritage of ours.   It stands out in bold relief upon every page of that thrilling and truth-telling bloody history.   We talk loud and long and enthusiastically about our political and religious liberties— our proud Republican institutions ; and our Revolutionary fathers.   And indeed, their chivalrous deeds of noble daring are the just themes of praise and song, among all the babbling tribes of earth.   But do we suppose for a single moment, that they ever could, or ever would have succeeded, but for the influence and interposition of our Revolutionary mothers ? No ! never.

What are the well attested historical facts, in the case ?   Most clearly that not only our Revolutionary mothers and wives and daughters and sisters of the heroes of '76, but also, that the ladies of the poor deluded tory party were almost 'to a man' heart and soul, devoted to the bleeding cause of National Freedom.   And as opportunity presented itself, they received the weary, worn soldier, with sweet smiles and

hearty blessings ; and at his departure, loaded him
down with benefits ; and cheered him on his perilous
weary way. These things should never be forgotten ; and I record them in my little book, for preservation. And so also, if our own patriot ladies generally took no part on the gory fields of battle, they
did more by encountering their privations and hardships, not only without murmurings, but with cheer-
fulness ; and that is the best part of it.

With an unsleeping vigilance, they watched every
movement of the common foe, and contrived some
way to communicate to the army the result of their
own private observation. Some of the British officers
had quartered themselves upon one Mrs. Lydia Dar-
ragh, who, somehow, understood that a deep-laid
plan was matured to surprise the beloved Washington,
and capture his gallant little host at a single dash.
Taking a pillow-case on her arm as if going to purchase a little flour, she managed to pass the guards
safely and unsuspected. Reported to Washington
the mode of the intended attack, and hastily returned
and went about her business as usual. Gen. Washington immediately changed his front of operations
so that when the attack was made, our boys were all
ready, willing, and waiting to give them a warm reception ; such an one as they had never before received, and never desired to receive again ; for they
were repulsed with great slaughter ; and routed,

horse, foot and dragoon.   Perhaps the success of the
Revolutionary war, was suspended upon this single
heroic effort or timely interference of female influence.   The ladies—and the American ladies, forever.
On another occasion of equally thrilling interest,
during the Revolutionary struggle of our gallant sires,
our Southern forts were threatened with a sudden
bombardment from a large fleet of War vessels; and
traitorous Tories had somehow communicated to the
fleet that our forts could offer no resistance, having
not a single yard of flannel, for cartridges ; nor had the
colonies the means to supply them.   These were in
very deed 'the days that tried men's souls. '   In this
dark hour of peril and conflict, our Revolutionary
mothers called a meeting, if possible to devise some
means to meet the pressing emergency.   They had
neither the means, the time, nor the implements to
manufacture flannel, to meet the demand.   What
should they do ?   Was it indeed true, that 'Where
there is a will, there is a way ? '   Yes, so it proved
to be on this occasion, as the record shows ; for, in
the midst of their dark musings, a bright idea entered the imagination of one of the ladies, when she
exultingly exclaimed, why, law bless me !   I have a
flannel skirt on, that will do for some—and so have
I ; and I ; and I too, joyfully responded they all.
Cheered and animated with the thought that had
just inspired them, they quickly dispersed, to accom-

plish that which they had just conceived. And in 'double quick time' they sent their husbands and their brothers a good supply of the much needed article ; which sent joy and gladness to the hearts of their friends, but death and gall to their adversaries. For when Sir Peter Parker (who had traitorously been informed of their utter destitution), bore down upon them, and opened a very deadly fire, vainly anticipating that an easy and safe conquest would close 'the grand drama' he found to his utter discomfiture and confusion, that 'our dogs of war' not only barked, but bit most sorely ; tore away the seat of his unmentionables, and made him a stranger to easy sitting ever afterwards.

He hauled off, as best he could ; dreadfully shattered and chagrined. And when he learned the history of this affair, he very sagely concluded and said, 'It is perfectly useless to war with a nation of such Patriotic ladies.' Aye, aye, sir ; you are very right in your conclusions ; as the record very clearly shows. Why, even the old Quaker lady, became so imbued with the spirit of the Revolution, that when her son caught the patriotic enthusiasm, and shouldered his gun to take part in the glorious strife, she gave to him her parting blessing ; and with it, this significant piece of advice.

Well, Nathan, if thee must go, never let me hear that thee is wounded in the back. Such then, were

the ladies of the Revolution.   No wonder that with
such mothers and sisters, with such wives and daughters, our Patriotic sires prevailed.   Female influence
marks every page of that most trying and perilous
period in our National existence or being.

And yet how little do we hear in our public haran-
gues or history, of their deeds of noble daring.   Are
gentlemen so deficient in their perceptive faculties,
that they cannot see these things?   Or are they too
modest to avow them? No! not altogether; for one
of our sweetest poets has sung their praises in rich
and beautiful poetic numbers—thus:

OUR REVOLUTIONARY MOTHERS.

O Pilgrim mothers! few the lyres,
   Your praises to prolong;
Though fame embalms our Pilgrim sires,
   And trumpets them in song.
Yet, ye were to those hearts of oak,
   The secret of their might;
Ye nerved the arms that hurled the stroke,
   In that long, bloody fight.

The fire of Freedom warmed each breast,
   Through many a weary day;
While pillowed soft in dreamy rest,
   Our infant fathers lay.
Ye taught them when their simple prayers
   Were breathed beside your knee,
The lessons which in after life,
   Were bulwarks of the free.

Ye taught to spurn the tyrant's chain,
  And bow to God alone;
Ye kindled in *their* hearts the flame
  That trembled in your own.
And though ye sleep on some bleak shore,
  Your names shall awe impart,
Your requiem—the ocean's roar,
  Your shrine—a nation's heart.

What a beautiful and what a well-deserved tribute. And I could not deny myself the pleasure of embalming their history in the pages of my little book, in connection with General Washington.

Little girls and young ladies, little boys and young men prepare yourselves for great events, and great events will prepare themselves for you.

My patrons will excuse me for this little digression —I trust. And now to extend this chapter a little, I will here treat you to a

NATIONAL HYMN FOR A 4TH OF JULY CELEBRATION.
Air—Auld-Lang-Syne.

Hail! hail! all hail the glorious Fourth, that gave a nation birth,
The brightest civil diadem, the richest boon of earth;
And never let this Natal Day be lost or turned aside,
To keep it up the good old way be every freeman's pride.

And never let them be forgot the sires from whom we came,
Whose blood-stained footsteps marked their way to glory and to fame;

And never let them be unsung who join in glorious strife
To plant the tree of liberty poured out the crimson life.

No, never let it be forgot, the price that freedom cost;
But pledge to each our lives, our all, it never shall be lost;
Let us preserve inviolate the legacy in trust,
And hand it down all bright and fair to those who follow
    us.

The East—the West—the North—the South we hail as
    brethren dear;
But claim the right as freemen should to speak out plain
    and clear;
Should e'er our country beat ' to arms,' we'll seize our
    muskets bright,
And like *brave* WARREN we will seek the hottest of the
    fight.

And though we sometimes disagree, no one has cause to
    fear,
The institutions of our land alike we all hold dear;
' This is the land that gave us birth, here we shall live
    and die,
And if one-half are deadly foes, will some friend tell me
    why?'

O, then away with bitter words, we all in heart are *one*,
United by the dearest ties the stranger sire and son.
Then hail! all hail! the glorious Fourth that gave a nation
    birth,
The brightest civil diadem—the richest boon of earth.

NOTE.—This was regarded as being a very fine poem in the day of it. If I misconceived the facts in the case, all I have to say is that it is vastly more honorable to be too charitable than too censorious. And if I did nothing to inspire the late terrible war, I made a full hand to suppress it when it came upon us, that's all.

I will now close this chapter with an

EPITAPH

for the tomb of Joseph Hannegan, a Revolutionary soldier, whose funeral oration I had the honor and pleasure to pronounce.

Beneath this stone an aged veteran lies,
Who early fought for ' freedom's golden prize,'
And lived to see her Eagle, Stripes and Stars
On every sea the pride of ' gallant tars.'

In seventy-six he joined ' the martial band,'
For liberty he fought with sword in hand,
Hunger and toil in common was his lot,
Which he endured, fought on—and murmured not.

Kings vainly boast ' the right Divine ' to reign,
All men by birth equally obtain,
Each patriot—the young—the older man,
Fought for this *truth* with our *loved Hannegan.*

Three-score and ten he more than lived to see,
Honored by all as he indeed should be,
How *sweet* his rest! ' the prize was nobly *won,*'
He *boldly* fought—he *sleeps* with WASHINGTON.

NOTE.—Approved or censured—appreciated or not, what I have written—I have written, and shall kindly and patiently abide the issue—and pass.

CHAPTER XII.

THE WAR OF 1812-14 AND GENERAL JACKSON.

The embargo times, and the war times of 1812 are still fresh upon my mind. Preparatory to the war was the embargo act to call in our own vessels, and to keep our money and our means at home. Our privations, of course, were many and exceedingly severe. We used pumpkin and sugar-tree molasses, sage and many other domestic teas, carrot, pea, and rye coffee, almost exclusively. Our mothers submitted to it without a murmur, because the rights of the country required the sacrifice. We paid from $1. 75 to $2. 00 per bushel for corn, and from $ 14 to $ 18 per barrel for flour, and hauled cordwood from eight to twenty miles for $1. 50 to $2. 00 per cord. I drove a team with wood many a day and night at those rates. We would start for Portland, a distance of twenty miles, at sunset, drive all night, and get into market at early dawn or sunrise, and if we met with a ready sale, home at early bedtime in the winter; otherwise, at a very late or rather early hour on the next morning. I have been so overcome with fatigue, and cold and broken rest, that I have

dropped my knife and fork a dozen times while eat-
ing my supper, my good mamma standing by me all
the time to cheer, and comfort and feed me. I
have traveled many a mile in a profound sleep by
the side of my oxen, got hold of the bow, lost myself,
woke up and found myself at least a mile ahead, and
all this for a mere pittance, hardly enough to 'keep
soul and body together.' Then a naked crust of
bread was sweeter than the richest bridal cake I
ever tasted, and that is saying a great deal. Year
after year the early frosts cut off our crops, and we
had to depend on southern corn, which we had thus
laboriously to obtain. Talk about hard times, who-
soever may, we don't know *here* in the west at this
time, the *first single letter* in 'the hard times alphabet.'
These reminiscences bring tears of gratitude to my
eyes at this moment. And but for the benefit of the
seaboard and her inexhaustible fisheries, I see not
how we could have possibly survived total starvation.
Our country, however, produced potatoes, peas,
beans, and garden vegetables in a fair abundance,
and we were able, by a great deal of hard labor and
economy, to keep up a fair dairy, and sheep to furnish us the materials for winter apparel, which our
mothers and sisters carded by hand, and spun and
wove at home.

The music of the spinning-wheel,
The shuttle and the loom,

greeted us from early dawn till nine or ten o'clock
at night. I fancy I see—I hear it now, and I am
young again—back to the days of youth and child-
hood—back to the dear parental hearth—parental
care and protection, and the fanciful contemplation
is mournfully sweet to my heart.

But the embargo times were succeeded by others
more severe and trying. Our husbands, sons, and
brothers, either by 'drafts' or 'enlistments,' were
torn from home to meet death, perhaps,

> On the field of battle,
> Where blood and carnage clothe the ground in crimson,
> Sounding with death-groans.

I shall never forget the time when an express was
sent into my neighborhood, post-haste, one Sabbath
afternoon, for a draft of so many to be made, forthwith, and to be at Portland on the next day, 'armed
and equipped for military duty.' The British fleet
lay off in sight, and an attack upon the beautiful
city of Portland was reasonably anticipated. That
was a time that tried men's souls. Some responded
to the draft cheerfully, and seemed eager for the
fight. Others ingloriously paid almost any price
for a substitute. And my lady's brother, Benjamin,
at a good round price, took the place of one less
courageous and less patriotic, perhaps, though, it
must be admitted that circumstances alter cases.
If ever I longed to be a man, it was then, when I

was hardly thirteen years of age. Bright and
early on Monday morning, our brave boys bade a
hasty adieu to home and friends, and amid tears
and blessings took the line of march for the post of
danger and death, to defend their common country
or die in her common cause. But so it was, after
lying off in sight for some time, and no doubt, by
some means or signals, ascertaining that we were
ready to give them a *warm* reception, they abandoned the intended expedition, and hauled off to
other fields of operation, and many of our valorous
men returned home after an absence of several
weeks, vexed that they had *missed* a fight. I more
than once visited what is call Portland Neck or
Promontory, when its forts and barracks were
swarming with men 'with nodding plumes and coats
of uniform.' I hear their drums and fifes, I see their
then marshal tread and evolutions, and catch the
glowing enthusiasm, while thus I write, as in the
days 'Lang Syne.'

When the startling intelligence swept over the
land, that the city of Washington, the Capital of the
Nation, was taken and pillaged, 'the hearts of patriots died within them.' I could name many that I
now see in my mind's eye, as they mournfully
walked the street, or, gathering together in little
groups, to counsel each other upon the sad and disheartening intelligence. I recollect, too, some of

the anti-war men, who seemed to exult that they were not committed. And with great complacency, as though they were sages and Solomons, they would, with seeming delight, 'cast into their teeth,' I *told you so.* Many a wakeful, restless night have I spent, dreading the consequences, wishing that I had the power to avenge and save my country, and praying God to interpose in our behalf. And when I learned that the next attack would, in all probability, be made upon New Orleans, and General Jackson had charge of her defense ; every night at my youthful prayers, (for I was taught never to close my eyes in sleep without prayer,) yes, every night I prayed for General Jackson, of whom I knew nothing up to this time. Every patriot eye was turned in that direction, and New Orleans was the engrossing theme of thought, of conversation, and of inquiry. Between five and six weeks after the battle of New Orleans, the glad, the overwhelmingly joyful news was heralded through Maine by government expresses on horseback. Put your horse through at the top of his speed, as far as he can go, and then turn him out and mount another. 'Uncle Sam' will foot the bill, seemed to be the instruction. Intelligence on a joyful theme like this could not be disseminated through the land in less than five or six weeks ! Now it can be done in about as many

seconds of time ! ! ! What an age of improvement
and progress, truly.

The joyful intelligence of New Orleans reached
me thus. I was at school, about one mile from home,
and about the middle of the afternoon, Josiah Walker,
a dear cousin of mine hove in sight, on his return
from Portland, with his oxen and sled, a handkerchief tied to the top of a long stake, old 'staf and
bright ' going it at the speed of 'double quick time, '
and he proclaiming at the top of his voice every few
minutes, 'General Jackson has whipped the British !
General Jackson has whipped the British ! ! ' The
whole school was perfectly electrified, my own heart
beat quick and free, the teacher ran out to make
inquiry, and learned that an express of that kind had
just been received at Por.land. On went Josiah,
and in came the teacher, announced the joyful news,
and turned us all out in a hurry ! and such another
scampering I never saw. 'Without stop or let ' I
hastened home at the top of my speed, and nearly
out of breath, I burst open the parental door, and
exclaimed most unceremoniously, as best I could,
General Jackson has whipped the British ! General
Jackson has whipped the British ! ! O, I was perfectly frantic with delight ; almost too happy to live ;
and recounting the scene I weep too much to write,
and must pause to give vent to my feelings, pay a

6

tearful tribute to the past, and a grateful one to the God of nations as well as of men.

Such a meeting together of patriots, such rejoicings I never before, **or never since,** saw or heard. The valleys and the mountains echoed back joy and thanksgiving and praise in every direction. And from that day to this, no living man ever occupied so large and so warm a seat in my affections, as a military or political man, as General Jackson.

GEN. JACKSON'S BIRTH-DAY CELEBRATION.

The first birth-day after his death, was on the Sabbath; and I was requested to select a text, and pronounce a sermon suitable for the occasion, which my heart of course, felt more than willing to do. A very large concourse of people had assembled together, to participate in the mournful, pleasant exercises of the day. I selected for my text 'whom having not seen, ye love.'

None I believe, took exceptions to my text after my application of it. It was regarded generally, I believe, as being decidedly one of my very best efforts. I concluded my address with a 'bran, splinter new poem' for the occasion, which seemed to take all with a very general, and very agreeable surprise. And here I present it to your consideration, for your entertainment and benefit.

ODE

TO GEN. JACKSON'S RELIGIOUS BIRTHDAY CELEBRATION.

Air—at pleasure.

Hushed be 'the music of the spheres' let freemen's grate-
    ful lay,
In one, loud chorus fill the earth, on this auspicious day !
Throughout the land let old and young, 'the lovely, and
    the fair, '
To pay 'a tribute' to true worth, their grateful hearts
    prepare !
My countrymen, with hearts all warm, we meet to cele-
    brate
        The birth-day of our Jackson dear,
          Jackson the good and great.

In seventeen hundred sixty- seven (1767), Andrew the
    great was born,
Just seventy-nine (79) eventful years, this precious, Sab-
    bath morn.
Long did he live to bless our land, and vindicate her
    rights !
        Now gone to his reward in heaven,
          To reap untold delights.

When 'savage war' and dread alarm were heard all o'er
    the land,
To quell those foes 'away down south' who led our mar-
    shal band ?
Who met 'the red man' face to face, his country to de-
    fend ?
        Go ask the tribes who with him fought
          Along 'the horse-shoe bend ! '

Tallapoosa will tell of gore, and Tallahassee, too,
'Twas a *sawauna* peace, returned through Jackson, unto
    you;
'The red men' and 'the red coats' too, found Jackson
    'full of fight,'
        He always left them in their gore,
        Or on the wings of flight.

Brave Jackson met 'proud Packingham' and all his
    vaunting host,
The 'beauty and the booty' saved, and drove them from
    our coast;
Valor and wisdom, ever marked each move in his 'war
    scenes,'
        The proudest victory ever won
        Was that of New Orleans.

Behold him in 'the forum' fair guiding 'the ship of
    State'
Where 'all the nations' own his skill, and all pronounce
    him great;
His chief desires he lived to see, accomplished to his
    mind,
        His dear, loved country and himself,
        He then to God resigned.

In peaceful slumbers soft and sweet, beside his faithful
    wife,
He rests in hope, till both shall wake to 'everlasting life;'
The 'conqueror of the conquerors' a greater victory won,
        When he subdued frail human self,
        Through God's beloved son.

The glory of his 'marshal tread,' the 'civic wreath' of
    fame,

Are vanity and dross, compared to his late Christian
    name;
The 'scroll of fame' shall long record the greatness of
    his name,
        Firmness and truth, and 'honor bright'
        And Jackson, are the same.

A name to freemen ever dear, to tyrants, death and gall,
Give us such men to guide the State, be this the prayer
    of all !
Farewell, great Jackson, words can't tell how dearly
    loved thou art;
        O, may the firmness of thy mind,
        Inspire each freeman's heart !

Then hush 'the music of the spheres' let freemen's
    grateful lay
In one loud chorus 'fill the earth' on this auspicious day !

In his latter days, General Jackson became deeply
pious, and joined the Christian church. His note to
me, which you will see elsewhere, is richly seasoned
with grace ; and its perusal cannot fail to gladden the
heart of every true child of God.

I will introduce you to it, by and by.

And now in all humility and meekness, may I not
ask, have I not kept myself pretty well 'posted up'
in the history and the wars of the country ? And
do not the two last poems abundantly sustain the
record ? Well, little boys, I did not gain all the in-

formation which I have turned here to such a good account, by strutting the streets with a cigar in my mouth, nor by loafing around liquor saloons, or any other evil retreat; but by a wise and judicious application of all my spare dimes, to the purchase of good books, and all my leisure hours in their perusal; as elsewhere, stated more fully. Compare your course and your pleasures, your honor and your fame, with mine; and then say, does it pay to live a virtuous and useful life? Does it, indeed?

And here is where the rum and tobacco questions come in again with good telling effect. Will you profit by it?

I will fill this page with one of my 4th of July volunteer toasts, as was usual in former times.

> General Jackson now and ever,
> He would not let the Union sever;
> In 'the forum' and 'the field'
> His country's rights would never yield.
> Now that he fills 'the chair of State'
> His acts proclaim him truly great;
> When having run his appointed race,
> May another good citizen take his place!

This toast was responded to, in the good old way, by 'three guns and nine hearty cheers.'

Now I ask, not to please myself, but to benefit you, is not that some, for a poor boy, a getting up in the picture? And does not the end truly justify the means?

O, boys, boys, make men of yourselves, instead of 'dandy fops,' will you?

A LOCK OF HAIR.

I was always a great admirer of General Jackson, although I never had the pleasure of being introduced to him. When lying sick, at Nashville, I addressed to him a short note bespeaking a lock of his hair, as a memento of him, &c.

True to his general character, he 'promptly' addressed to me, the following chaste, beautiful and friendly Christian note:

Honored and Dear Sir, Agreeably to your request, with great pleasure I herewith enclose to you a lock of my hair. My extreme illness prevents me from writing much at this time. I am quite unable to wield the pen successfully, though I have made the effort. I thank you Sir for your very kind, personal regards towards me; and wishing you a long, useful and happy life, and a blessed immortality beyond the grave, where, through the atonements of a crucified Redeemer, I hope to meet you and see you, face to face, I subscribe myself, yours most sincerely,

ANDREW JACKSON.

To which, among other things, I responded thus :—

Most honored Sir, **I do** declare
That silvered lock **of your** pure hair,
Which you in answer to my prayer enclosed to me,
Of tokens all, it is most **fair,**
Yes, ' fair as fair can be.'
Where' er in life, my lot is cast,
I'll call to mind the fruitful past;
Your mighty acts, so many, vast,
As on that lock I gaze.

I' ll prize it high, I' ll hold it fast,
Till sighs are lost in praise.
O, let us daily ask for grace
To run throughout 'the Christian race '
Then if we see each other's face,
Not once below,
On Zion' s mount, thrice holy place,
We each shall see and know.

Sweet is the hope, the joy complete,
When pious friends shall yonder meet,
And flit along the golden **street,**
In robes of white;
And loud hosannas there repeat
With pure delight.

Our friends who have before us gone
Shall join with us in the glad song,
Yes, we shall each sing loud and long,
When all meet there.
Your 'faith in Christ ' I see is strong,
In answer to my prayer.

May you wind up life's grand career,
All full of comfort and good cheer,
And Angels 'round your bed appear
As you depart,
To guard you safe to yon bright sphere,
So says my heart.

A. J. COTTON.

This little poem brought forth the following editorial in the columns of a New Albany Journal, as elsewhere introduced, and will, I think, do well to repeat, for 'good reasons :' 'Judge Cotton is certainly a rare genius and always had a great passion for poetic composition. He is now getting quite old, yet, he writes poetry with the beauty and elegance of earlier years. His style is peculiarly his own, and some of his productions have found their way into some of the first magazines of the country. We remember that once on a time, he wrote a little sonnet, that would have done credit to Tom Hood ; all about 'a lock of General Jackson's hair' which the old General had enclosed to him in a letter from the hermitage.' What ! A. J. Cotton, a poor, obscure little boy, rise up to correspond with General Jackson, and win such an editorial puff'! Here boys, is where the rum and tobacco comes in again. Don't you see

6*

it? and don't it pay? and pay well, too? Now don't it?

Any one can see that letter and lock of hair, by calling at my pretty residence, Yarmouth, Me.

CHAPTER XIII.

Whenever any 'big doings' were being had in my county, I was generally on hand as an officer or with a poem, or a speech. This chapter will be devoted to Agricultural Fairs.

ODE

To the first Dearborn County Agricultural Fair; and which will be more or less applicable to Fairs generally.

The Dearborn County Fair shall usher in my song;
Please lend me your attention, it will not take me long;
So my humble muse 'tune up,' 'wide awake'
In truth and rhyme, a synopsis now take,
    Of the Dearborn County Fair.

There were geldings and mares, Jennets too, and Jacks,
Roans, dapple grays and sorrels, creams, chestnuts and
    blacks;
All sorts and all sizes, sleek'd off for a show;
Some were most beautiful, and others so, so—
    At the Dearborn County Fair.

There were oxen and cows, calves, sheep and fat hogs,
Polar chickens and brahmas, and plenty of dogs;
There were farming utensils, a grain-sower and plough;
And threshing machines, that did it up—how,
    At the Dearborn County Fair.

There was grass-seed, wheat, potatoes and corn,
Fine apples and peaches 'as ever were born;'
There was cabbage and beets, and radishes, too,
Sweet potatoes and pears, most pleasing to view,
    At the Dearborn County Fair.

There was, let me see ; but I will not tell all,
Lest your patience I weary, and my story forestall.
But butter ; O, bless me! as yellow as gold,
As sweet as pure honey, admired, but not sold,
    At the Dearborn County Fair.

The finest of bread, too, to match the fine butter,
You'd eat it with pleasure, and for more you would
    mutter;
There were stockings and shoes, and carpets and quilts,
Counterpanes and blankets, the work of no jilts,
    At the Dearborn County Fair.

The patterns were fine, and the needlework, too,
Such as our ladies know just how to do;
Crysanthemums and dahlias, and roses, in bloom;
And geraniums, too, all rich in perfume,
    At the Dearborn County Fair.

There were saddles and bridles, harnesses, whips,
And I venture to say, that not one of 'em rips;
They were tasty and neat, and made a fine show;
They must have been extra, talked about so
    At the Dearborn County Fair.

And buggies and gigs, if you ever wish to ride
Easily, gracefully, and with honest pride,
Just purchase a carriage of Helper & Co.,
Encourage true merit, and thus add to the show,
    Of the Dearborn County Fair.

But the ladies ; O, bless them ! so lovely and fair,
All neater than pinks, were the finest things there;
Their presence and smiles, send joy to the heart ,
May they meet us next year, and all take a part,
      In the Dearborn County Fair.

Such a show once a year, must do us much good,
Henceforth we shall 'farm it ' much more as we should;
Emulation and pride, will 'the masses' inspire,
Next year we will 'come it ' infusing new fire,
      At the Dearborn County Fair.

Two full acres in one, and far better than that,
If we keep our farms neat, and keep our land fat;
And horticulture, too, neglected too long,
Shall inspire my muse, and continue my song,
      Of the Dearborn County Fair.

May neatness and flowers, instead of rank weeds,
The garden adorn, then rich its proceeds;
Men, women and children 'fly about ' and prepare,
And next year without fail, be sure to be there,
      At the Dearborn County Fair.

Everything we make, eat, drink or wear,
Should be greatly improved, at our next County Fair.
Then hand in your names, and 'fork over ' your cash,
And there will be neither 'poor stock ' nor poor trash,
      At our next County Fair.

This ode seemed to be a very timely and acceptable offering, and won for me much credit and praise.
I give it a place in my sketch book, that all the little
boys may see how easy it is to tell a story in 'poetic
numbers' when you know how; and that all the

Agricultural interests of the country, **may** avail themselves of the benefit of my suggestions. 'To do **good and** communicate, forget **not**; **for** with **such** sacrifices, God is well **pleased.** ' Bible.

ODE TO INDUSTRY.

Sung at the first Agricultural Fair, of Dearborn **Co.** and ordered by **vote, to be** published **with the proceedings,** together with a **vote of thanks, to** the author.

APOTHEGM.

'Cursed is **the** ground, **for thy sake.** ' Gen. iii- 16.
Air—Auld Lang **Syne.**

Cursed be the **ground in mercy cursed. for fallen sinful**
  man;
And who that rightly understands, **does not approve** God's
  plan.
This is a life of constant toil, hereafter we shall **rest;**
And he who is most **active here,** shall there enjoy **it best.**
The cultivation of the earth, **through toil,** and sweat **and**
  sighs,
Is heaven's choicest, richest boon, all blessings in disguise.
The thorns and thistles, that we dread, which **choke the**
  growing grain,
Give exercise to willing hands, and **health and peace**
  maintain.
The idle and the dissolute, most sure to ruin run,
Who proves a burden to himself, oft as the rich man's
  son.
The toiling millions of the earth, enjoy night's sweet
  repose,

All strangers unto wakefulness, and other people's woes.
Then push along 'the mighty plough' cheer up! go
    Charlie ! go !
And men and boys, in merry mood, keep moving with
    the hoe,
And shove, and shove the plane along, ye artists of the
    land;
'Tis by your strength and industry, we ever more must
    stand.
The smith, beside his glowing forge, his anvil and his
    vice,
With brawny hands and merry brow, will serve you in a
    trice.
The politician 'wide awake' will smile, and scrape, and
    bow ;
And pledge you much some other time, to get your vote
    'just now.'
The student, at his musty books, with scientific fires,
Propels the car along the track, and thoughts, along the
    wires.
The soldier, at the cannon's mouth, death staring in his
    face,
'Mid clashing steels defends his land, from ruin and dis-
    grace.
The sailor, 'ploughs proud ocean's foam, ' no timid heart
    has he;
To gather wealth, he boldly braves 'the perils of the sea. '
The doctor mounts his trusty nag and on through sleet
    and snow,
He hastens to the sick one's couch, to soothe 'the wail of
    woe.'
The lawyer, and the ermined judge, well versed in legal
    lore,

By mental toil are known abroad, and famed 'from shore
    to shore. '
The minister, divinely sent with messages of love,
Points to 'the house not made with hands' eternal, and
    above.
'The music of the spinning-wheel, ' the shuttle and the
    loom,
Would sweeten all the ills of life, and chase away the
    gloom.
The kitchen and the parlor, too, ye lovely and ye fair,
Becomes you all, and will repay your presence and your
    care.
All, all on earth, should active be, the Sun and Moon and
    stars,
Keep whirling through the void immense, Earth, Jupiter
    and Mars.
Then push along the mighty plough, cheer up ! go Char-
    ley ! go !
And men and boys in merry mood, 'keep moving' with
    the hoe.

The great object of this poem, is to reconcile men,
women and children, to their lots of toil and conflict.
When mankind had become fallen and debased, a
paradisical state of idleness would have been ruin-
ous to him ; and God, in mercy, turned him out to
cultivate the earth ; and to earn his bread, by the
sweat of his brow. I hope all the little boys will
receive comfort and profit, by its perusal. This was
thought in its time to be a very happy hit ; and won
for me unmeasured praise, at home and abroad.

The savings of rum and tobacco, applied to the

purchase of good books, furnish the means for all this usefulness and honest fame. Does it pay, boys? or rather does it not pay well? Try it boys!

ODE TO PROGRESS.

Sung at the Dearborn Co. Agricultural Fair. 1854.

APOTHEGM: 'Up and at it.'

Air—Auld Lang Syne.

What great improvements mark the age in which we
    chance to live;
O, who would then an idler be, and not his tribute give?
Then 'up and at it' little boys! nor lose one single min-
    ute;
You all should make this world the better, for having
    once been in it,
How things have changed, and been improved, within
    a few brief years!
It swells the heart with gratitude, and calls forth hearty
    cheers.
When we were little boys and girls, some fifty years ago,
We used our tinder, flint and steel, 'twas click, and puff
    and blow;
But now, we take a bit of pine, and split it fine and then—
Into a 'chemical compound' the ends we just dip in,
A little friction then will raise 'a blazing torch of fire;'
Perhaps we hardly need expect to carry that much higher.
We used to rake our hay by hand, our ploughs were
    made of wood;
Now, they are made of polished steel, and horses, rake
    so good.

Horses and oxen used to draw our produce and our
    goods,
O'er mountains, hills and valleys, too, through slashes
    and the woods ;
But now our famed 'old iron horse' comes snorting on
    the track,
Swift as the winds, our goods and all, he'll take right
    there, and back.
To cross the ocean, years gone by, consumed long, wea-
    ry months ;
But now, our gallant ships of steam, will take you there
    at once.
Expresses, too, we used to send on horseback, through
    deep mires ;
But now, they go with 'lightning speed ' on telegraphic
    wires.
Improvements must, and will go on, though telegraphs
    are some,
They'll surely be behind the times, in fifty years to come.
'The master spirit of the age ' O, who, who shall it be ?
Let every youngster here respond, it may, it shall, be me!
Then 'up and at it ' brave, young men, nor lose one sin-
    gle minute ;
You all should make the world some better, for having
    just been it.
When Franklin sent his little kite and bottle to that
    cloud,
And filled it full of lightning red, it was a conquest proud;
But O ! how little did he dream, that electric fires
Would e'er diffuse great truths abroad, on long, suspended
    wires.
Developments in moral truth, in science and in art,
Forever lead to others sure, of one great whole, a part.

Then 'up and at it' one and all, nor lose one single
    minute ;
You all should leave this world much better, for be-
    ing ever in it.

The following record soon appeared in the papers,
to wit :

'At a meeting of the board of directors, of the
Dearborn County Agricultural Society, the following resolution was unanimously adopted. *Resolved,*
that Rev. A. J. Cotton be, and he is hereby presented with a life honorary membership, in this society.
The 'Ode to Progress' was made by him, and sung at
the third Annual Fair of said society. 1854.

            J. W. Eggleston, President.

Francis Worley, Secretary.

Boys, look at that, and then at this ! Will you ?

A POETIC ADDRESS.

Pronounced at the Dearborn Co. Agricultural Fair. 1857.

'A farmer's forest life,' I own, has many charms for me ;
Give ear my friends, awhile, and the wherefores you
    shall see.
He first selects 'a tract of land' midst birds and blossoms
    fair,
Then settles in his anxious mind, to make his home right
    there.
Erects a neat log cabin, out in the open woods ;
Has neither stock nor cash, perhaps, nor much of house-
    hold goods.

But the hope of better days, gives strength unto his arm,
And 'at it' now he goes, to clear him up a farm;
His viands, coarse and common, and scanty, too, at that;
But instead of getting poor, he is rather getting fat.
Toil gives it 'a good relish' and sweetens his repose,
'For change and recreation' to hunt awhile he goes;
With rifle on his shoulder, and with Jowler at his side,
The space between him and his home, is soon made very
    wide.
He scours both 'hills and dales' for turkeys, bears and
    deer,
Returns at night quite weary, with 'lots' of hearty cheer ;
    perhaps.
His wife and little ones, smiling and all fair,
Now hasten out to meet him, and soothe his brow of
    care;
His tea 'perhaps of sassafras, of spicebush, or of sage,
Has long been waiting, but goes 'first-rate' I'll venture
    to engage.
And then, he has fine 'nuts to crack' at eve, or in foul
    weather:
His overalls, were sometimes made of yellow tanned
    'buckskin leather.'
His neighbors, all are very kind, each feels himself a
    brother;
For lack of schools, his children are all taught at home
    by mother.
He has 'a little patch for truck' though rather rough at
    first,
He cannot do without it, and have it he will, and must.
In time, it makes a 'pretty garden' full of 'sweet shrubs
    and flowers,'

Where he 'his wife and children' spend many happy
    hours: or at least, should.
As time rolls on, his fertile fields, and herds and flocks
    increase,
His cribs and stables well supplied, his yards, with poul-
    try, pigs and geese;
And as occasion may require, he'll slay, and cook and
    eat,
For pure domestic happiness, his life is 'hard to beat.'
Tis true, we had our troubles then, and you all have them
    now,
So happiness at last depends upon the mind I trow;
We were quite happy in those days, in hope of better
    times,
And made a shift to get along, and live without 'the
    dimes.'
For fifty cents, or less, my friends, we'd toil all day in
    summer,
And keep as busy too, at that, as any little drummer;
We'd sell our corn at sixteen cents, not always sure of
    that,
And pork, one dollar twenty-five, that was all
    rolling fat.
With tow and linen pantaloons, and hats of 'chip and
    straw,'
We lived upon equality, and seldom 'went to law.'
Our corn we ground in mills, by hand, to make our
    'bread and mush;'
And often went abroad all barefoot, O hush now, hush!
    hush!! hush!!!
Our wives, our sons and daughters, could fare but little
    better,
'Tis true what I am telling friends, 'true to the very
    letter.'

Just fifty cents per week, was all 'our gals' could get,
And thought a chance like that, a very happy hit.
Eight cents per pound for butter, and eggs, four cents
    per dozen,
The highest price one could obtain, from merchant,
    friend, or cousin.
A striped linsey home-made dress, they'd 'cut a merry
    dash,'
Which they had spun and wove and made, without one
    dime in cash.
Our teachers took their 'hard earned' pay, in corn and
    pork and beef,
A little linsey, now and then, would give them great
    relief;
They'd board around from place to place, nor murmur at
    the fare,
Would bow at your devotions, and often 'lead in prayer.'
The Preachers, bless 'em! one and all, went forth 'both
    far and near,'
To warn poor sinners of their ways, the saints to 'feast
    and cheer;'
They'd 'go through thick and thin' through mud and
    sleet and snow,
You'd always 'find them at their post' if you yourself
    would go.
Their churches were 'a neighbor's cabin' upon some
    ridge or creek,
With chimneys built with 'cats and mud' for then we
    had no brick;
With 'puncheon floors' all under foot, and clapboards
    over head;
And lights for windows 'paper oiled' I've witnessed
    what I've said.

All clad in coarse, plain home spun, and 'neater than a
    pink, '
He takes his family to church to 'worship God and think '
About his future home, in climes more bright and fair,
Then consecrate himself anew, by faith and humble
    prayer.
Begins the week quite much refreshed, in body and in
    skill,
Assured that God is with him now, he sinks into his will.
His wife and children, are all now, to him surpassing
    fair;
Delighted with his forest home, finds peace and comfort
    there.
And oft, with one child in his arms, another on his back,
He 'cuts across ' the forest wide, along his blazed out
    track,
To spend a happy evening, with some dear, kind forest
    friends;
Then with 'a lighted torch ' his homeward way he wends.
Upon his safe arrival there, he strikes him up a fire,
How happy we shall be my dear, when we have neigh-
    bors nigher !
Talks o' er his pleasant visit, then bows himself in prayer,
And soon in peaceful slumbers, forgets both toil and care.
The wolf, the bear, the panther, quite oft beset his track,
The very first he knows perhaps, they' re well nigh on his
    back;
But God preserves him strangely, his wife and bub and
    sis,
I' ve witnessed in my time, dear friends, such thrilling
    scenes as this.
Still to our homes we' d fondly cling, and grub and hoe
    and plow,

Perhaps we all were happier then, than any of us here,
  are now.
We had fine peaches, 'rich as cream ' to eat, to sell and
  dry,
To the memory of those days, I pay 'the tribute of a sigh.'
Still these are better times, by far, and happier we should
  be,
Such great improvements in my time, I never thought
  to see.
We used to deal alone on time, and paid up, in produce,
To ask the cash no one presumed, unless 'to play the
  deuce. '
Now, 'ready cash ' is 'all the go ' for labor, goods, or
  wares,
And lo! my friends, we have fine '.Agricultural Fairs. '
What mighty changes for the better these forty years
  have wrought !
To you, young friends, 'a rich inheritance, to us, most
  dearly bought.
Young ladies, and young gentlemen, you scarce 'begin
  to know '
The dangers, toils and hardships, we had to undergo
In clearing up the country, that's now so bright and
  fair;
Which you from us inherit, without a seeming care.
Our roads were rough and muddy too, our mills so far away
It took one full day to go, and sometimes two, to stay;
Your roads are fine, and turnpiked, too, your mills are
  just in sight,
Where you can go and get your grist, and back before
  'tis night;
You have your 'railroads and canals, ' your telegraphic
  wires,

Fine churches, too, to worship God, with carpets, bells
    and spires.
You have fine houses, and fine farms, barouches, chaise
    and gigs,
And dress in silks and broadcloth, and feast on dainties
    and roast pigs.
Cleave to these farms, young gentlemen, improve and
    keep them nice !
They'll yield you health and plenty, and keep you out of
    vice;
The rush for learned professions, is rushing into strife,
And oft is purchased at the price of happiness for life.
'The brawling politician' lives in a constant muss,
To keep up fair appearance, must keep an endless fuss;
His life is restless as can be, nor dare he once deny it,
If any of you doubt it, friends, just sell your farms, and
    'try it.'
The lawyer, too, has strife on strife, the doctor has
    great care,
Be the success what e'er it may, or practice anywhere:
Both are essential callings, though, and oft they 'make
    it pay,'
But would you once exchange with them, say farmers,
    say ?
You are thrice happy as you plant, and happy as you
    sow,
Or as you follow the good old plough, or cradle, reap or
    mow;
Richer by far, than mighty kings, in palace, hall, or dome,
As you chant your merry anthem, your own sweet har-
    vest home.
·Huzza ! huzza both men and boys, for the farmer and
    mechanic,
7

They both are 'independent men' and no bank money
    panic
Can e'er disturb their sweet repose, or tarnish their good
    name,
They're loved and honored in their lives, and in their
    deaths the same.
Where are those hardy pioneers, who early settled here?
Most of them gone, and very soon, the last will disappear;
I too, am frail, and getting old, and soon must pass away,
Well, 'be it so' I am content, since I have seen this day.
Forty long years have well nigh fled, and years of change
    and toil,
Since I first settled in your midst, and purchased of your
    soil;
'Twas then 'a howling wilderness' with scarce one stick
    amiss,
Nor did I then begin to dream, of seeing a day like this.
I leave the country much improved, in 'science and in
    art,'
And trust I've been no 'hanger on,' have acted well my
    part.
May smiling peace and plenty, forever bless this land;
For 'truth and right' dear friends, forever firmly stand !
  Is the wish and prayer of your speaker.

I need hardly say that I sat down in a perfect
shower of vociferous and prolonged cheering. Does
it pay to be useful and true ? This has been pronounced to be the very greatest, grandest and truest
poem of the kind that the world ever saw. And it
will be heard or read with deeper and deeper interest, the farther 'we glide down the stream of time.'

And now, by way of concluding this chapter, let me say, that I   won a premium of $15. 00, for the best essay on Agriculture, against two well educated and professional gentlemen, of high standing.   The State board published it in their annual report, and sent to my address a very pretty and well bound book, containing it.

Now is that not something to be justly proud of? A poor, self-made man, to compete successfully with two college learned and professional men ! Is that nothing to be courted and admired ?   Do I merit the epithet of an egotist, for writing out my own true history ?   Egotism, indeed!   I indignantly repel the charge.   I have no vanity to flatter.   I am a frail, feeble, old man, and soon, very soon shall have passed away.   I strike for higher game, to encourage not only the little boys of this generation, but the little boys for many generations, to come.   I fully believe, that God gave to me my talents to be im-proved—gave to me my very wonderful experience, and has most kindly preserved my life, to write it out ; and opened up the way for me to publish it to the world.   I know I thus write to glorify God, and to do good to my race, and not for vain glory.

Those who have never achieved anything either good or great, in the world, nothing to inspire their own esteem, or the esteem and good opinions of others, may turn up their noses, make up wry faces,

and cry, egotism! egotism! egotism! to their own
heart's content; while I go about my way, and
'pursue the even course of my affairs' happy and
content.   By dint of close study, hard and constant
application, I know that I have performed wonders;
and you all know it too.   I give the little boys and
young men the benefit of my example, hoping that
they will as far outdo me, as I have outdone you.
And that is saying much ; and here I leave you, for
the present.

CHAPTER XIV.

SABBATH SCHOOL POEMS.

ODE TO SABBATH SCHOOLS.

Air—Auld Lang Syne.

CANTO I.

Awake my muse, the Sabbath Schools
    Now claim a lay from thee;
And teachers, as 'your work of love,'
    My offering is free.

Soon will these boys become 'young men,'
    These girls 'young ladies too,'
Their moral culture for the time,
    Entrusted is to you.

The first impressions that are made,
    Are lasting as the mind,
See to it then that every one
    To virtue be inclined.

O 'tis indeed a tender charge,
    To have the care of youth,
To lead them from the 'haunts of vice,'
    In all 'the path of truth.'

And yet it is a 'pleasing task,'
    Those lessons to impart,
That strengthen and improve the mind
    And purify the heart.

Eternity alone can tell
　　The good you will have done,
Then onward roll the enterprise,
　　Rejoicing every one.

CANTO II.

Now scholars dear I pray you all
　　Hallow God's holy day,
And love your school, your teachers, too,
　　Who often for you pray.

Let God be first in whom you trust,
　　And he shall guide you well,
What you should do, and what eschew,
　　His word and spirit tell.

The precepts that are clearly taught
　　In God's most precious book,
Would comfort and sustain you all
　　Though heaven and earth were shook.

I think alas ! how soon will pass
　　The pleasing scenes of youth,
And what I now do say to you
　　You 'll find to be a truth.

This world of woe through which you go
　　Is full of 'pits and snares,'
Unless you daily 'watch and pray'
　　You 'll fall in unawares.

The fatal bowl which blights the soul,
　　O ! dash at once away,
'Twill ruin all, both great and small,
　　And drain the purse to pay.

The brightest hopes, the fairest flowers,
　　Before it droop and die,

Then say dear youth I 'll touch it not, '
  Nor I— nor I— nor I—.

You will succeed in rapid speed
  To rule in Church or State,
O ! try and qualify yourselves
  For trusts that are so great.

Our stripes and stars will very soon
  Be trusted to your care,
May you be ready to receive
  And keep them bright and fair.

And may the God of peace and love
  Direct your roving feet,
And in the 'house not made with hands, '
  May we at last all meet.

CANTO III.

Now friends and neighbors one and all
  Keep up 'the Sabbath Schools ; '
They will do more for tender youth
  Then arbitrary rules.

They 'll save your sons and daughters fair,
  From ruin and from sin,
To rear them up just as you should
  You early should begin.

No better means, no fitter times
  Instruction to impart,
As 'Sabbath Schools ' directly tend
  To train the infant heart.

They everywhere are gotten up
  By men both good and wise,
O ! cherish and sustain them well
  And rich will be the prize.

Last year the friends of the first Congregational Sabbath School, Yarmouth, Me., chartered a steamboat, with a Brass Band and banners, for a pleasure excursion and picnic, out among the islands of the beautiful bay, and came to anchor at Peak's Island, a very justly celebrated summer resort, lying off some four or five leagues from Yarmouth harbor. Rev. Mr. Bartlett, Pastor, extended to me a kind invitation to accompany them, and to address his little group of happy children; but there being such a multitude of other picnicers on hand, it was found to be quite out of the question to organize. All enjoyed themselves, however, most hugely, in little private groups; and hence the address which I had prepared, did not come off. But I have concluded to publish it, in my little, pretty book, for the benefit of all immediately interested therein; and I inscribe it to Sabbath Schools generally. With slight alterations, it will serve on all such occasions, through all coming time. And hence I send it abroad in my little book, as part and parcel of my own humble record. And here it is, for you.

ODE FOR A SABBATH SCHOOL PICNIC CELE- BRATION.

Air—‘ Hearken ye sprightly.’

The Sabbath Schools, hope of the church and nation,
Have pressing claims upon our time and money;
And here we come with music and with banners,
To cheer to duty.

Then children come ! come one and all together,
Let us make merry this delightful morning;
The earth looks gay, clad in her robes of floral
           To greet us welcome.

To this sweet grove, we come with waving banners
To enjoy the fragrance of these verdant bowers ;
And to inhale the cool, refreshing breezes
           Which come to cheer us.

Here we may talk and laugh, and romp at pleasure,
And run and jump, and swing and whoop and huzza
Without restraint, and be in perfect order
           For picnic past-time.

'Twill do us good, relax the weary muscles,
Give tone to mind, enfeebled by close study;
'The bow long bent, becomes unnerved and useless'
           When most you need it.

Your kind good teachers fain would make you happy,
And see you healthy, loved and good and useful;
Else they would not have gotten up this picnic
           For your amusement.

Enjoy it well, just as it was intended,
And then resume your studies in good earnest;
Be kind in school, and thus repay your teachers
           For their pains taking.

      Soon you will step upon the stage of action,
      And take a part in 'life' s eventful drama,'
      See to it then, that all be made the better
           By your example.

Drinking saloons, those sinks of dissipation,
With horror shun at once, and on and on forever;
   7*

Touch not the ruby wine, 'it stingeth like an adder, '
    Thousands have proved it.

O ! search the scriptures, instead of sickly novels,
They'll make you wise, and guide your wandering foot-
    steps
In paths of peace, which lead to bliss immortal;
    When life is over.

Remember too, that one and all are destined
To live forever in 'the land of spirits;'
So live on earth, that each may gain a mansion
    High up in heaven.

    A cheering word to 'officers and teachers,'
    Yours is a work an Angel might admire;
    To start the young off in the right direction,
        For lives of honor.

    And parents, too, should take a biding interest
    In Sabbath Schools, those 'nuseries of virtue,'
    Visit them oft, thus show their deep devotion
        To good instruction

    But after all, the place for youthful training,
    Is right at home, by father, and by mother;
    Let infant minds be taught to love the Saviour,
        In the home circle.

    God bless the children, is my heart's desire,
    May they grow up pious men and women;
    And better serve their day and generation,
        Than did their fathers.

    I hardly know how to conclude my story,
    Such is my love for Sabbath School instruction;
    But time forbids, and this must be sufficient
        For this occasion.—Amen.

LITTLE WILLIE, THE CRUSHED BOY.

I select this little, pretty and most pathetic and instructive Sabbath School story, for the pleasing entertainment, and for the mental and moral improvement of my little readers. Here it is for you. Read it, will you? And at your leisure commit it to memory; for declamation, on some Sabbath School celebration, as also for the entertainment of your parents and teachers, and little friends, generally. The Lord bless all the dear little children, while I proceed to pen the little article referred to.

And here it is : —

A great crowd of people had gathered around
A small ragged urchin, stretched out on the ground
In the midst of the street ; and some cried, for shame !
And others, can any one tell us of his humble name ?
For that mangled boy, now bleeding and still,
Was all that was left of bright little Will.
A great heavy cart had come rattling that way,
Where Willie and others were busy at play;
And the poor little fellow, now stretched on the stones,
Seemed only a mass of crushed flesh and bones.
But still there was life, and the doctor then said,
'We must take poor Willie and put him to bed;
He must have all the care we can possibly give,
Who knows but that poor Willie may live ? '
But alas ! for the lad, he had no nice pretty home,
He lived in an alley, in a little dark room;
And his mother, hard toiling from the earliest day-light,
Had often no supper to give him at night.

But joy, for poor Willie ! for not far away
From the place where all crushed and bleeding he lay,
Is a very large house standing back from the street,
With everything round it, so quiet and neat,
Which many good people had built in his name,
Who healed all the sick, from heaven he came;
And who promises blessings, that ever endure,
To those who are kind to the sick and the poor.
So there in a room, large, cheerful and bright,
Little Willie was laid on a pillow so white.
The walls with bright pictures, were covered all o 'er,
Willie never saw such a nice place before;
Long rows of small beds, with tables between,
All beautiful and nice, and painted with green.
And so many children all sick, but so bright,
Willie forgot all his pain at the beautiful sight;
But the poor boy suffered most terrible pain,
When the good doctor came to see him again.
Those poor mangled limbs, he said 'the next day,
I must bring my sharp knives and cut them away. '
Oh ! how could he bear it ?   Oh ! what should he do ?
So small and alone, could he live to get through ?
Even if he should, he nevermore could run
And play with the boys, as before he had done.
Poor Willie !   he felt that in all that great City,
There was no one to help him, or even to pity.
It was night—and all was so dark and so still,
Save the low moanings from poor little Will;
When a dear little girl, in the very next bed,
Turned 'round on her pillow, and lovingly said,
Little boy, what 's the matter ? are you very ill ?
O, yes, said poor Willie, but what is worse still,
The doctor is going to hurt my legs so

To-morrow, I never can stand it, that I just know.
But Jesus will help you, said dear little Sue,
He suffered and died, poor Willie, for you;
The child was astonished, and thus made reply,
Why Susie ! who 's Jesus, and what made him die?
Oh Willie ! how sad ! I thought every one knew,
You don 't go to Sunday School then, poor Willie, do you ?
No, I never have been, the boy made reply,
But tell me of Jesus, and what made him die ?
Well, Jesus, said Susie, came down long ago,
From heaven above, to save us from woe;
Was a very kind and most dutiful child,
Just as little as we, but so gentle and mild !
And when he grew up he went through the land,
And healed all the sick, by the touch of his hand;
And he took little children right up in his arms,
To bless, and to save them from sin' s fatal charms.
But some wicked men, caught this Jesus one day,
And beat him, and mocked him, and led him away;
Nailed him to a cross, which they made out of wood,
Oh ! wasn 't that cruel, when he was so good ?
How he must have loved us, to die on the tree,
Said Willie, if dead, how can he help me ?
I 'll tell you, said Sue, 'though he' s in heaven,
In his word, a promise to all he has given;
Whenever we need him, he 'll come to our aid,
So cheer up little Willie, and don 't be afraid.
Very often he comes to the hospital here,
Though no one can see him, all feel that he is near;
I know, for I 've tried him again and again,
He helps us bear sickness, and sorrow and pain.
O ! how good, said the boy, with a tear and a sigh,
But I am so small, that he might pass me by;

O, I 'll hold up my hand, just so he can see,
And then do you think he'll come round to me ?
O, yes, that he will, he is now passing by,
Perhaps to take you, right home to the beautiful sky;
When the bright sun shone on his nice little bed,
The hand was still raised, but Willie was dead.
The sad look of pain, had gone from his face,
And the sweet smile of peace, had taken its place;
Far away in bright heaven, that beautiful land,
Kind Jesus had seen little Willie 's white hand.
Come unto me, was the kind message given,
And he 'woke in the morning, with Jesus in heaven.
All who may read this sweet story, assuredly will see,
That Jesus and mercy, and heaven, are free;
May all who of Jesus ' great mercy have heard,
Like dear little Willie, take Christ at his word !

Is not this single story worth more than the price
of my book ?

CHAPTER XV.

TEMPERANCE POEMS.

FOR A FOURTH OF JULY TEMPERANCE CELE-BRATION.

Air—Auld Lang Syne.

THE Temperance Ball, the Temperance Ball!
    Let 's keep it on the roll,
Till doggeries, those sinks of woe,
    Are crushed from pole to pole.

And every 'Still Tub' in the land
    Be knocked the 't' other side up,
And spill the swill that makes the '*bane*'
    'That sparkles in the cup.'

The streams of death that issue forth
    From every smoking Still,
Are blighting all our brightest hopes,
    And all our prisons fill.

O! think it o 'er—mature it well;
    That 'fip' upon thy corn,
May crush the hopes of many friends,
    And leave them quite forlorn.

Our fathers fought, and bled, and died,
    Despising ease and gain;
And to be worthy of those sires,
    We all should do the same.

Shall we claim kindred to those men,
  Who live alone for self ?
And scatter woe, disease and death
  To treasure up our pelf ?

Nay; starve 'the Worm ' of every Still—
  Convert your grain to bread,
And send it round from door to door
  Till all the poor are fed.

Ye topers and ye tipplers, too,
  Though late, you are 'in time '—
The second Declaration 's here—
  O ! come you up and 'sign ! '

Throw off at once the galling yoke
  King Alcohol imposes;
He drains your purse—pollutes your breath,
  And *burns* to *red your* NOSES !

'Hope of my country, ' dear young men,
  O come ! and 'sign the pledge :'
'Twill save your country, save you, too,
  As thousands can allege.

Disease and death lurk in the bowl,
  The mind 't will shatter, too;
How can you then preserve the trust
  That soon will fall to you ?

The destiny of 'Church and State '
  Will in your hands be placed,
And if unholy, drunken men,
  Both sure will be disgraced.

Our Stripes and Stars will very soon
  Be 'trusted to your care;
May you be ready to receive,
  And keep them bright and fair.

Let old and young—let boys and girls,
  Like 'Hannibal,' come up
And swear eternal hate to him—
  The FOE that 's in the cup.

Ye blushing Fair lend us your aid—
  Your 's is a potent charm—
You rule the men who rule the State—
  You can avert the harm.

O ! never let it be forgot,
  The price that freedom cost;
But pledge with us your lives, your all,
  It never shall be lost.

O wield the power which Nature gives,
  To dry these founts of woe—
The sorrows of 'a drunkard 's wife, '
  O may you never know.

Then roll it on !—'that Temperance Ball, '
  And keep it on the roll,
Till doggeries, those sinks of woe,
  Are crushed from pole to pole.

DIVORCE.

LOOKING over my court journal of 1839, I find also the following memorandum:

H——VS. H——.—BILL FOR DIVORCE.

TESTIMONY.—Plaintiff was married to defendant thirteen years ago, and took with her about two thousand dollars worth of property and money; got along swimmingly and happily for several years, at which time defendant contracted habits of intemperance, and latterly, for months at a time, has scarcely drawn a sober breath. Many have been his acts of cruelty and personal violence to his said wife, knocking her down with chairs, dragging her about the room by the hair of her head; kicking and breaking her ribs, until her life was well nigh despaired of; the property all squandered away, sold under the hammer for liquor bills and bad debts, contracted under its influence; even the little pittance which his said wife would earn with her needle or at the wash-tub, was often violently seized and expended in drams. Plaintiff lived in constant fear, and was in imminent danger of life and limb if she longer attempted to live with her said husband.

MANY WITNESSES.

Decree, of course, entered accordingly.

The investigation all through, was one of deep and thrilling interest. My heart bled at every pore during the painful recital, and I made the following entry in my 'note book' at the time, which all the curious can see at any time by calling on me:—

O! intemperance! intemperance!! How many and how sad are thy trophies! How many tender ties hast thou severed! How many bright hopes hast thou obliterated! How many kind confiding hearts hast thou crushed into the very dust! How many kind parents, good husbands, fond wives, dutiful children, true and kind friends, hast thou disappointed; made wretched, and sent sorrowing to the grave! How many millions hast thou squandered away! Surely, misery and death thou spreadest 'broad-cast' every where, and virtue and happiness fly at thy approach. How long shall these things be? These were my reflections, as judged and noted down in my journal nearly twenty long eventful years ago. And my sluggish muse, animated and inspired by the painful reminiscence above referred to, is in for a lay; and Pegasus, becoming restive and impatient to be off, I drop him a slack rein, and here goes:—

With grief and indignation, too, I heard this tale of woe,
And tears of deep-felt sympathy, all gushing forth did
> flow;
It did not well become a judge, full well, my friends, I
> know it,
But as my heart so freely bled, I must and could but
> show it.

I thought of early and bright hopes, now sere, and cold,
> and dead,
And bliss so rich and full and sweet, that had for ever
> fled;
A home that once was full of joy, now full of grief and
> pain;
And as I mused, I deeply sighed, and freely wept again.

With broken heart and mind and health, this once most
> happy bride
Now seeks to be released from him who was her former
> pride.
Her children and her numerous friends, deposing, inter-
> cede—
That she no longer would be safe—they all as one agreed.

What were the reasons, do you ask? These were, in
> fine, the sum—
Neglect, abuse, and poverty, all caused by using rum.
'Rum and ruin' are allied, and will forever be;
Yet, there are men who peddle grog when these results
> they see.

Their hearts are steeled and steeped in sin, they care not
    for the ruin;
They spread 'broad-cast' throughout the land, nor for
    the soul's undoing,—
Monsters they are in human shape, who will just for the
    dimes,
Prepare and instigate their friends for tragedy and crimes.
I'd sooner beg my daily bread, be clad in filthy rags,
Than roll in wealth thus illy gained, admired by fools or
    wags.
O rum, what ruin thou hast wrought, how fearful is thy
    reign;
And nought can check thy mad career, nought but the
    law of Maine.
The waste of morals, time and means, and of domestic
    peace,
Since prohibition was annulled has been on the increase.
When will the people all declare such shall no longer be ?
Time will determine that my friends, and you must wait
    with me;
And put your shouldder to the wheel and speak and
    write and vote,
And soon you'll see the temperance ship well manned
    and all afloat.
Roll on reform—thy mighty car shall triumph in the end;
The peace and safety of the State on these events de-
    pend.
O parents rally while you may, and save your daughters
    dear,
From woes that are unutterable, and from the scalding
    tear:
And save your sons from infamy, yourselves from sad
    despair,
And God in mercy interpose, is now my daily prayer.·

What languague shall I use, what metaphors employ,
To paint rum's waste and havoc, of morals, means and
 joy ?
The naked skulls and skeletons, of all by liquor slain,
Would form a pyramid that would pierce the clouds that
 send us rain.
Could all the tears just caused by rum, unite from shore
 to shore,
They'd form a cataract more grand than Niagara's
 mighty roar;
And sighs commingled all in one would silence deep-
 toned thunder: (*perhaps*)
And that these things so long have been (*allowed*) is to
 my soul a wonder.

Crape every planet, every star, blow out the burning sun,
Hang all the heavens in sack-cloth too, and you have
 scarce begun
To paint the desolation, the mourning and the woe,
That from the liquor business has, and will forever flow.
This is no fancy sketch, dear friends, but demonstrative
  ⋅ truth,
Intended to arrest the mind and save the precious youth.
Ye rulers and ye judges too, why stand ye here all idle ?
Up, up, and chain the monster, curb him with bit and
 bridle.

Say unto him: 'thus far thou mayest, but farther canst
 not go,'
King alcohol, thou mighty nag, hold up—whoa ! whoa ! !
 whoa ! ! !
Thus shall ye 'serve your day and age,' and all by rum
 made wretched;
And millions yet unborn, with them shall call you blessed

THE DRAMSELLER'S LOOKING GLASS.

A TEMPERANCE DITTY.

Air—'Old Dan Tucker.'

Of all pursuits that have ever been,
　Retailing grog, is the meanest thing;
'T has caused more misery, pain and woe,
　Than ever from one source did flow.
　　　Chorus:

'Git out of the way' all you Dramsellers,
You 've ruined 'lots of clever fellows.'

　You 've severed in twain husband and wife,
　　Made happy homes all gall and strife;
　For rowdy, drunken sprees at night,
　　Put wife and children all to flight.
　　　Chorus.

You 've taken the shoes from poor women 's feet,
And the bread their children had need to eat;
　You 've robbed them of their scanty clothes,
　　And left them crying, and half froze.
　　　Chorus.

　You 've made sweet children beg and sigh,
　　Wrung bitter tears from their mother's eye,
As oft she heard them cry for bread,
　As hungry, they were sent to bed.
　　　Chorus.

You 've turned kind husbands into knaves,
   Made loving wives, most abject slaves;
You scatter crime, and want and woe,
   'Broad-cast' and thick, where e'er you go.
        Chorus.

You 're guilty of all kinds of sin,
   The meanest that has ever been;
You 've robbed the rich, and you 've robbed
     the poor,
   And drove the needy from your door.
        Chorus.

You ' ve robbed the strong of his strength,
   Then laid him down in the mud, full
     length;
And you 've left him there, to grunt and roll,
   Like 'a filthy hog ' in an old mud hole.
        Chorus.

Now he that peddles grog, through the land,
   Should on his forehead wear this brand
'I 'm a dread Maelstrom, in life's rough sea,'
   As 'a deadly asp' let all shun me.
        Chorus.

The grog that makes men spew and reel,
   Prompts to murder, rob and steal;
To grieve their friends, they seldom fail,
   And their career oft ends in jail.
        Chorus.

There 's better work for you to do,
   Than 'peddle grog' which all must rue;
It covers one 's friend all o 'er with shame,
   Empties his purse, and blasts his fame.

Come sign the pledge, all you dram-sellers,
And ruin no more of 'the clever fellows.'

From pole to pole, the news shall spread,
That children nowhere cry for bread;
When dram-sellers throughout the land,
No longer in our way shall stand.
Come sign the pledge, all you dram-sellers,
And ruin no more of 'the clever fellows,'
Come, sign the pledge, like 'clever fellows,'
And help reclaim all poor dram-sellers.

This ditty was originated by Dr. Garretson, of Dearborn Co. Indiana. Corrected, enlarged, and improved.

I now propose to close this chapter, with one of the very flattering, public compliments, that have been accorded to me, specially as a temperance orator. I quote from a Western Journal, of the 'long, long ago.' Then, I was in my prime of life, voice full, clear and musical; and I was well posted, and full of heart and hope, and in good health. Now, I am a frail, feeble old man, the merest shadow of my former self, and out of speaking gear, altogether. But to have won such high sounding praise in my palmiest days, is pleasurable to contemplate at life's closing scene. My little readers, it pays well. Will you try it? But here it is, for you, and may it do you all good, as it doth the upright in heart.

COMPLIMENTARY NOTICES.

'MR. EDITOR:—I see that my friend, Judge Cotton, is on the track for the office of Recorder, at the next election, and with characteristic magnanimity he assures us, that 'he has not taken the field to oppose any one,' and only asks, in turn, that none take the field to oppose him. This is generous, this is reasonable!

'Now, Mr. Editor, I am in for the Judge, decidedly; and, sir, if the idea of any man having claims upon the public for office, is not altogether inadmissible, I claim that Judge Cotton's claims to the office in question, are paramount to those of any other man in the country; and I am satisfied that facts will fully corroborate the assumption. Judge Cotton has been a resident of Dearborn county, I presume, some thirty-five years. Nearly the whole of the active, valuable portion of his life has been devoted to the interests of the county and State, and I may say, of the world; for the Judge's philanthropy partakes not of the selfish, or centripetal element, exclusively, but is essentialy diffusive in its character— a most harmonious combination of the centripetal and centrifugal forces. His energies have not been exerted in the accumulation of wealth, or for his own aggrandizement, but for the benefit of mankind. In the several capacities of teacher, minister, judicial

8

officer, and temperance lecturer, he has served his generation well and faithfully; and I venture to affirm, that in the prosecution of these various avocations he has spent more time, made greater sacrifices of personal ease and comfort, and surmounted more difficulties, than any other man in Dearborn county has done for such objects. And by far the greater portion of this labor has been performed without any hope of remuneration, except such as is a legitimate sequence of a life devoted to the cause of truth and humanity. And now, to sum up the whole matter, I must insist, that of all men in the county, Judge Cotton ought to be elected our next Recorder. His past valuable and unrequited labors demand it; pecuniarily he needs it; and surely a grateful and appreciating public will award it. So mote it be. '

'The meeting then adjourned, giving three cheers for Judge Cotton. We have been in agony about this matter, but the agony is over. Judge Cotton will sweep all before him, wherever he goes, like a mighty torrent. We say to our friends abroad, Judge Cotton is the man, without any more delay. No time is to be lost. We can elect him if there are a dozen candidates in the field.

In conclusion, we would say to the voters of Dearborn, 'go to work at once, and in earnest. Let the watchword be, JUDGE COTTON, VIRTUE and VICTORY!!!

'If the whigs, on a proper consideration of the matter, conclude to cast their votes for an independent democrat; I know of no one more capable, honest and available, than Judge A. J. Cotton, of Manchester. The high standing of the Judge as an honest man, good neighbor, and christian, points him out as the man for that high office. '

'The Judge was then called out to address the meeting. He begged to be excused, as there were a plenty of good speakers present, and as he had already, perhaps, addressed the audience a hundred times upon the subject, and that it would be peculiarly embarrassing at this time to impose himself upon the audience, many of whom had come from afar to hear another gentleman of known ability, of pleasing, graceful manners, and rich and flowing eloquence. But it was no go. *Cotton!* COTTON!! COTTON!!! was echoed through the hall most enthusiastically. There being no 'let up' the Judge responded to the call in one of his most amusing and happy strains, for some forty minutes. The vast assemblage was often perfectly convulsed with laughter; and anon they were as still as death.

'His temperance picture, which is purely original, was finely sketched, and told well upon the cause. 'It was rich as cream. '

' JUDGE COTTON'S POEMS.—We have once or twice announced the intention of Judge Cotton to

collect the most, if not all of his numerous fugitive
pieces which have enlivened the columns of news-
papers for twenty-five or thirty years. He is getting
old, yet he writes poetry with the beauty and elegance of earlier years. His style is his own, and
some of his ealier productions found their way into
the first magazines in the country. We learn that
a thousand copies of his book are already subscribed
for. We hope to hear of their early publication. '

'THE RULING PASSION STRONG IN DEATH.—By
the last mail we received a letter and a few verses
of poetry from our old friend, Judge ALFRED J. COT-
TON, of Dearborn Co., which will be found in another column.

'The Judge is certainly a rare genius—possessing
greater versatility of character than is often met with
in one man. He is a farmer, in a small way—a
preacher of the Gospel, a school teacher—a universal poet, for many years associate judge, under the
old regime, afterward probate judge, a patriot who
loves his country, a universal favorite at wedding
parties, in which he had a great run, and where he
officiated with entire satisfaction to the young folks,
more especially as he always accompanied the marriage notice with an appropriate verse or two of his
own composing.

'He always had a great passion for scribbling poetry, and we remember that, 'once upon a time, ' he

wrote a sonnet that would have done credit to Tom
Hood, all about a lock of Gen. Jackson's hair, which
the old general had enclosed to him in a letter from
the Hermitage.

'The last time we had the pleasure of meeting him
was at the people's convention at Indianapolis, on
the 13th of July last. We saw then that he was
rapidly passing down the vale of life, and that his
'work was about done.' May his end be peaceful
and happy.'

These flattering and honorable notices which have
been widely circulated through the periodicals of the
day, and, to which I might add many more of the
same sort, is to me rich reward for a lifetime devoted to the well-being of the community, in the midst
of which my pleasant lot has been cast.

CHAPTER XVI.

REMOVAL TO ILLINOIS.

I had intended to conclude my Indiana history, with another chapter, which I had carefully prepared ; but necessity compels me to omit it, altogether ; as it does a few other chapters.   Consequently, I leave old Dearborn, rather abruptly, and hereby invite my readers young and old, male and female, to accompany me to my new and beautiful home in Illinois ; for after having 'served my day and generation ' as best I could in Indiana, for 48 long, eventful years, for good reasons, I sold my pretty cottage home, and removed to Crawford Co., Ill., to spend the evening of my days with my married son ; my only surviving child.   My full history here would alone fill a large book.   I announced an appointment for my farewell sermon.   I had a very full and even crowded house.   The Lord stood by me, and we had a very fond and friendly parting.   On motion of my worthy friend, Rev. Dr. S. Flood, a surprise collection was taken up for my benefit.   The Dr. urging all to contribute freely and cheerfully ; since the citizens of Dearborn were justly indebted to me, not one single cent less than $10,000.00. For all his days he has 'gone about doing good among them.' Sixty dollars were raised just on the spur of the moment; showing, that I still lived in the hearts of the people, and that all my old friends were not taken prisoners of war, or slain upon the battle fields of the then late and bloody rebellion. With a sad heart, I tore myself away from friends and home, and in due time arrived at my new destination. The next day, Rev. Dr. P. Hale, a total stranger to me, called to greet me welcome to my new home, and to invite me to accompany him in his carriage to our quarterly meeting, to-morrow. Being very feeble and much fatigued, I promptly declined; said he, Rev. old Father Dollehan and Rev. Brother Richee, who heard you preach when you were out here to your son's a few years ago, sent me after you, and told me to be sure and take you along, and I don't like to go without you. My sainted, good lady prevailed upon me to go, saying, the Lord may have something for you to do. Well of course I went; found the conference in session; when these good brethren hastened to greet me welcome, and brought down Dr. Hawley, the presiding Elder, who said, I am right glad to see you, and wish you to preach to-morrow, at 11 o'clock. Thanking him kindly, I stated that I was utterly too feeble to preach, and if I were not, I certainly could not consent to occupy his hour on

the Sabbath.   Well, said he, the brethren all say you
must preach ; and if not to-morrow, do so this evening.
We shall have a full house, and I will help you out
the best I can, for I see you are in very poor health.
Now then what could I do, but to make the effort.
And if I ever felt that 'when I am weak, then am I
strong,' it was on this occasion.   The elder endorsed me fully and flatteringly, and all blessed me
most heartily welcome.   And thus the Lord gave to
me an open introduction to this very kind and strange
people, my new neighbors.   -

At our next quarterly meeting, the elder would
take no denial ; preach I must, and preach I did, on
Sabbath, and 'swung clear' again, as we preachers
say.   The elder again fully endorsed me, in one of
his happiest hits, and then called upon all the church
to join in a united prayer for my restoration to health,
for the edification and comfort of the church—Rev.
Dr. Hale leading in prayer.   And O ! what a prayer.
And how fervently and eloquently did he pray that
I might be spared to the church and the world, for
many years to come.   And O, how many and how
hearty were the Amens.   And there upon my knees,
I felt that prayer had prevailed with God in my behalf.   And there and then, a thrill of unusual power
perfectly electrified me throughout ; and I felt that I
was saved.   On my return home, I said to Mrs.
Cotton, my dear, I shall not die yet ; but live on a

while longer, in answer to prayer. That was about ten years ago, and all my friends here, say, that ordinarily I am good for at least a dozen years more.

So much then for praying faith. What saith it? If two 'or more' of you shall agree touching anything that they shall ask, it shall be done for them, of my Father, which is heaven. O, for more of living, prevailing faith! which laughs at impossibilities, and cries, it shall be done. Is not this a wonderful interposition of providence? and should I not record it to the praise of his grace, who says, ask and it shall be given to you? Subseqently, I attended camp meeting, at the instance of that same good old father Dollehan, who kindly invited me to take a seat in his carriage. On my arrival, the elder expressed great delight at seeing me, conducted me to good quarters, and would have insisted on my preaching to-morrow (Sabbath), at 11 o 'clock, had not the programme assigned to him a special subject for that hour; but he would waive the morning love feast, and have me occupy that hour. And he who said, 'lo I am with you alway' stood by me of a blessed truth; and we had a most precious season, specially and generally, at the stand and tents. When the Elder's hour arrived, it threatened heavy rain immediately; and the people began to scatter rapidly, when I incidentally said, 'I don't think it will rain here.'

8*

Whereupon the Elder proclaimed aloud, Judge says he don't think it will rain here ; join in faith with brother Cotton, keep your seats, and see what the Lord will do for us. All settled back into their seats 'and as sure as the Lord liveth' we had not a single drop of rain on any part of the encampment, although there was a heavy shower not 80 rods distant. This wonderful incident gave me great grace in the eyes of all this strange multitude. And thus most graciously and providentially, did the Lord open the way before me for good among this strange people. And I was looked upon from that day out, as something a little extra in my line. And it will not take you long to believe that fully. Immediately after breakfast Monday morning, father Dollehan hitched up for home ; and as we were very busy in shaking hands and pronouncing our 'good byes' Elder Hawley tripped up behind me, and tapping me gently on the shoulder said, Judge, I cannot let you go, without one more of your sermons. O, no, said I, we are all ready to start, and must be off immediately. I can't help that said he, the ministers have just held a consultation, and charged me not to let you leave until you had preached once more ; adding very pleasantly, I am the presiding elder, you know, and it is your duty to obey. I knew that I had made my mark, and a second effort would be to preach against myself; and how I did beg to be excused. Right then and there, what should Father Dollehan do, but say, Judge, I want to hear you again as much as any of them do, and don't mean to start, until you treat us to one more of your good sermons. And when I saw that there was no 'let up' I said, 'Lord help,' and went upon the stand in the midst of a good love feast season, during singing and prayers; and O! how the good Elder did pray for me. A text occurred to my mind, which proved to be a most felicitous one, and I had no sooner begun to open my mouth than the Lord began to fill it with 'words that breathe, and thoughts that burn.' And if ever a minister had his full armor on, I had mine on, of a blessed truth. Praise the Lord. Brother English our very able and acceptable circuit preacher, followed me with a very strong exhortation in which he said, 'when I heard the Judge yesterday, I thought that must surely be his very best sermon; but he has totally eclipsed himself, on this occasion.' And the Elder in his camp meeting report to our church journals, said, 'Rev. Judge Cotton, a local elder, who has recently settled among us, added much to the interest of the meeting, by treating us to two of his most novel, truth-telling and inspiring sermons.' Was not that a very high compliment, boys, from a very high source? How deservedly, those can best say, who were present on this most happy and delightful occasion. Shortly after, I preached at Robinson, my own county seat. The editor of the *Argus*, was present, and in an editorial, in his next issue said this:

Rev. Judge Cotton on last Sabbath, treated our people to one of his 'wide awake ' and very spicy sermons. The church was full to a perfect jam; and the Judge held them in profound silence, and with thrilling interest and delight, for just one full hour. It was indeed a rare treat to all present. The Judge always commands large and attentive audiences, because he always has something new and novel to say, and knows just when and how to say it. All hope that he will visit us again soon, and then quite often.

EDITOR.

That is quite glory enough; and I quit right here. Now perhaps, in borrowed phrase, I might just as well say here, as anywhere, that 'from a very humble and obscure beginning (as I have elsewhere stated), the little celebrity I have won as a minister, has been won by dint of hard study, close and continuous application, close observation, and close communion with God; having almost exclusively consecrated myself and my all, to the ministry in 'the morning of my days.' Starting out in my 'ministerial career' at an early and tender age, with such qualifications only as were common to all, an education which had little more than just fairly commenced under the disheartening pressure of many disadvantages; but eventually turned to some little account, by unremitted devotion to elementary books and private study in leisure hours, rainy days and long evenings.

But with a heart and a will to go forward in the work and mission I had assumed, I felt from the very first, and at every single step forward in my official duties, that something beyond the ordinary food and exercises of the mind, was absolutely necessary to prepare me for my 'pulpit duties' and responsibilities; that determined personal energy and application of efforts were absolutely and indispensably necessary for my success either to usefulness or 'honest fame' as a minister of the Gospel of Christ. And relying upon Divine aid, I did so apply myself, as all well know who are intimately acquainted with me. And without guide or model, with no books at first, except my Bible, my hymn book and my discipline. In the wilds of the West, surrounded by howling beasts of prey, I projected and explored my pathway, aping no man; but from the beginning to the end, I have been my own peculiar, original self in the pulpit, as in all the other duties and affairs of life. Yielding to the inexplicable yearnings of my heart, to be both good and useful, I have appropriated all within my reach for my own special aid and benefit, and advancement in my ministerial career—reading, writing, reflection, observation, experience, meditation and prayer, and all the energies of mind and body nave been invoked and applied to for light and guidance in 'my high calling of God, in Christ Jesus.'

The midnight lamp, or 'hickory torch-light' has often found me at my books and my prayers. Thought demanded materials, and ends exacted means. And without constant effort for mental growth and enlargement, all chance or hope of success was forever foreclosed. Such then were the circumstances of trial, of ignorance and want, under which I commenced my ministerial career. And although I have much to regret that my sermons have not been more spiritual, more eloquent and successful generally, yet I greatly rejoice that they have in some sense, and to a limited degree, been serviceable and acceptable to the church and to the world, and that I have never knowingly trifled with myself, or my high and holy mission, by 'handling the word of God deceitfully,' nor by attempting to turn it to worldly advantage or preferments, by perverting the tastes or tickling the ears of others.

Nay, I have rather sacrificed all my worldly hopes and aspirations, that I might make full proof of my ministry, and 'finish my course with joy.' I have not 'lied to the Holy Ghost' for worldly gains, or to please any man, or set of men for any personal effect whatever. And I am not conscious of any ambition or aspiration, unworthy 'the high and holy mission' of an ambassador of Christ. And as inefficient as my ministrations have been, they uniformly have been my very best efforts under all the circumstances. And I have often, quite often, been exceedingly joyful and happy, in their performances. In 'breaking the bread of life' to others, my own soul has feasted on the rich and heavenly repast; and the remembrance of those precious seasons, is sweet to my soul.

So much then in brief, of my ministerial career, which is in all human probability, about being wound up, and closed forever. And I am quite happy and cheered with the hope that I shall be enabled to 'render up my account with joy, and not with grief.' Yes, that I do, through mercy rich and full and free.

To God be all the praise, hence evermore. Hallelujah, Amen.

CHAPTER XVII.

CONCLUSION.

I now discover that I cannot possibly crowd all of my carefully prepared matter into my little book; and so I have concluded to quit square off right here, and close up the entire matter for the present; and reserve all the balance for another pretty, little book 'of the same sort' soon as convenient, should my present work prove to be a profitable and acceptable offering; otherwise, I have written quite too much already.

When the Saviour had about finished his great mission and ministry upon the earth, He said, Father 'I have glorified thee on the earth; I have finished the work which thou gavest me to do.' And now in all humility, may I not assume that these significant words 'in a qualified sense' will not inaptly apply to myself, and history? For have I not too, 'glorified God on the earth' by an early and almost entire consecration of myself, and my all to his cause and service 'in the kingdom and patience of Christ?' And now that I am well stricken in years, and my pretty book about ready for distribution, and the materials for the closing volume all well nigh prepared, with what propriety may I now also say, 'I have finished the work thou gavest me to do.' Alas! how imperfectly; but it is finished, and so it must remain forever. And after all my watchfulness and prayerfulness, I have written many lines which, dying, I fain would blast from the record, though I think in all truthful soberness, I can say, notwithstanding my foibles, my errors and my faults, there has never been in me 'an evil heart of unbelief, in departing from the living God,' since the day of 'my happy espousal of Christ and his cross.' Well, to be sure, 'what a mighty work did God assign to me!' Let me pause and think a little—my sermons, orations, Sabbath School and temperance addresses, are not told by hundreds only, but by thousands; yes, by thousands. Then I have published one large, miscellaneous work, called Cotton's Keepsake, which had a fine run in its day. And now, my sketch-book, &c., and I have on file, in manuscript, a history of slavery, from the day of its birth, to the day of its death. And O! what a history. Then I have 'The Heavenly Mariner,' an allegory, it would seem cannot possibly fail to serve and please. And several other good works, surely. But whether they ever go to press or not, time alone will determine. But at any rate, this announcement will tend to show that mine has been a very active, busy life. And then my writings for the Press, and my private correspondence, have been perfectly overwhelming. Meantime, I have been quite an extensive home traveler, have been more or less, in 24 of the States, off into the Canadas, and out upon 'the illimitable sea,' and 'far away.' Have seen all the great sights nearly in the country. William and Mary's college, in old Virginia, the Washington monument, in Maryland, the Rock monument, in Canada, ground out a poem on the summit of Bunker Hill monument, 'which see,' preached on the lofty height of Mount Abraham, 'see poem,' twice visited the White mountains, ground out a poem at the Niagara Falls, 'which see,' passed over the Lacine Falls in the St. Lawrence, near Montreal (a thrilling scene), have seen the Lewiston Falls, the Genesee Falls, the Falls of the Ohio river, the Robber's Den (rather a scary place), the Jackson monument, on the plains of secession, passed out to lake Ponchartrain, and over the battle field of New Orleans, and down to Fort Proctor, on the Gulf of Mexico. Now indeed, for a poor obscure little boy, have I not seen sights, and performed wonders worthy of publication to the world?

And then, too, I have worked my way up to an elder-ship, a judge-ship, a United States marshal-ship, an editor-ship, an attorney-ship, and an author-ship. And those who shall read my little book, can see ust how these great things have been accomplished.

And that is the main object I have in view, in sending abroad my life's humble and eventful history. And whether I make or lose, by the operation, the church and country will get the full benefit of my life and history. Now I can't believe that God in his providence gave me such a history to be lost. And hence I have written it down in a book, and leave the event with God and my friends, and abide the issue in 'good hope.' Now if I am providentially serving God in this matter, he will open the hearts of the people, and they in turn will open their purses cheaply and liberally, to sustain me in it. And if otherwise, what am I, better than other men? History shows that many of the world's greatest benefactors, have died in alms-houses, while some have 'begged their daily bread, through lands their valor won.'

And now, just a word or two about my new and happy home, and I am done for the present. When I look back to my humble beginning in life, think how much good I have tried to accomplish, how many and great have been my $500.00 donations to Moore's Hill college, and my gratuitous services, and then think what a pretty, neat, little cottage home, with such very romantic and beautiful surroundings, and such a superior wife to take care of it, and me, too, I say in my heart most gratefully, surely I have not served God, his church, or my country, in vain; surely not. But look out for something rich, on this score in my next forthcoming book, which I think must, and will be more interesting than this one, the very cream of the whole story. I hardly expect to live to execute it. If not, my good lady will. Indeed, she made the arrangement, furnished the means, and is the real publisher of this; a real smart, capable, business lady. And I hopefully commit her to God, and my friends. Sketches in her very pious and eventful history, as an instructress, a seamstress, principal nurse of the Chelsea hospital, matron of the Bridgewater almshouse, Mass., and a missionary teacher to the freedmen of the South, and the very flattering notices accorded to her, in the journals of the day, are all held in reserve for my IId volume. My golden wedding poem and Christian song of deliverance, set to music, will for the present be distributed in ballad form, as heretofore ; but will together with a most telling and beautiful poem in relation thereto, by the venerable G. W. Chapman (the prince of Acrostic writers), as also my war poems, including a eulogy and lament upon the life and assassination of the greatly beloved and deeply lamented Abraham Lincoln, the crowning subject, and the masterly effort of my humble muse, must go over. And of course every body will want a copy of my IId volume ; but must wait patiently for it. In which due mention will be made of my 70th birth-day present of the splendid watch I sport as a donation from the citizens of old Dearborn, as well as the magnificent public dinners served up for the occasion by my cherished pupils and life-abiding friends, Ralph Collier, corresponding editor of the Press, and his most amiable and interesting better half, Mrs. May Collier. And other grateful tributes to my old frends of Dearborn and Crawford Counties, must live in my heart until I can transcribe them into my forthcoming interesting, pretty little book. Surely my humble life has not been a failure, but 'a glorious success.'

And now, Lord, having written finis to my little book, what await I, for my hope is in thee.

Let me go—my soul is weary of the chain, that binds it
    here ;
Let my spirit bend her pinions to a holier, brighter
    sphere.
Earth, 'tis true, has friends to bless me with their fond
    and faithful love;
But the hands of Angels beckon me on to brighter worlds
    above.

Let me go—my heart has tasted of my Saviour's wondrous grace;
Let me go where I shall ever know, and see him face to
    face.
Let me go—the trees of heaven, rise before me waving
    bright;
And the distant, crystal waters flash upon my ravished
    sight.

Let me go—for songs seraphic, now seem chanting
    from the sky;
'Tis the welcome of the angels, which e'en now are hov-
    ering nigh.
Let me go—they wait to bear me to the mansions of
    the blest;
Where the spirit worn and weary, finds at last its long
    sought rest.

Even so, 'Come Lord Jesus, and come quickly ;'
'Happy if with my latest breath, I may but gasp his
    name,
Preach him to all, and cry in death, behold ! behold the
    Lamb. '

BENEDICTION.

And now 'a kind and parting word' to the little girls and
    boys,
'Seek God in early life,' my dears, for pure substantial
    joys;
Young men and women, soon you'll be, and fill our va-
    cant places,
I trust with pure and honest hearts, and smiling, happy
    faces.
And serve your day and age, as we have done before,
My warmest blessings to you all, and I can say no more;
May heaven's kind, protecting arms forever 'round you
    dwell,
And now my little dear, young friends, receive my fond
    farewell.

THE AUTHOR.

I shall not index this volume of my work, for good and conclusive reasons. The reader can pencil mark, and index those items deemed worthy, as he goes along.

Persons desiring a copy of my book, can obtain one, by calling on the publishers, B. Thurston & Co., No. 111 Exchange St., Portland, Me., or by enclosing to them $1.10 will receive the book by return mail, post-paid.

SUPPLEMENTAL.

A CARD.

My friends, please read this little card, and I will
not inflict a speech upon you. Here it is, in my
new, pretty book, which I now place in your hands
for inspection, and intend to make you a present of
it, as 'A Keepsake' with one single condition, which
this card will fully explain. You will discover at
sight, that my publishers, B. Thurston & Co., have
executed my work, in a very neat and workman-
like manner, a clear, full type, for the accommoda-
tion of the old folks, and that, too, upon excellent
paper. And also, that Small & Shackford, binders,
have performed their part most handsomely, too.
And it affords me pleasure to say, that all these gentlemen, the proof-readers, included, are exceedingly
pleasant and agreeable gentlemen to deal with.

Having no ministerial field of labor to occupy, I propose to travel about a little, preach and
lecture, as I go, and to dispose of as many of my little books as I well can, while passing around from
place to place. My good lady will aid me in their
distribution. But let no one do me the injustice to

9

say, Judge Cotton has turned out to be 'a book ped-
lar,' at last. If however, ' a good book is the best
household treasure,' there can be nothing disrepu-
table in peddling them. But as I am rather an odd,
original genius, I tell the same story altogether in a
different manner. I say, that 'I am passing around
to hunt up my available and reliable friends, to make
them a present of it, as a Keepsake, in remembrance
of me. And on the frontispiece page, is a blank,
which reads thus, 'A Keepsake, presented to——.
By the author.' Fill the blank with your own name,
or let me fill it, for you, and that will make it all
right. But lest I should be imposed upon, I ask my
friends to pass over to me just $1.00 in token of
their genuine friendship; then I place their names
upon my list of friends, in a little book, which I take
along with me for that special purpose, and forthwith make them a present of one of my pretty, little
books, in token of my love and gratitude, to them.
A fair exchange is even, up and all the way round.
If you wish to procure one of my books, on these
terms, say so at once and cheerfully; if not, say so,
frankly, without the least embarrassment, and with
the kindest and best of wishes, I will bid you a pleasant good-bye, and depart in peace. And thus you
see a story can be told just as well one way, as another, if you only have ingenuity to know how to do
it. And I cannot dispose of a single book on any

other terms, not one. And now, if you admire my fifty years in the West, my snake, wolf, bear and panther stories, as I trust and hope you will, please take a copy under your arm, and step right over to your neighbors, at your earliest, convenient season, and say to them, 'have you seen Judge Cotton's pretty book ? You ought by all means to procure a copy of it, the best book for a family, in the market. You might just as well look for a needle in a hay stack, as to try to hunt up a nicer and better little book.' That is very well said, and I am much obliged, for it is indeed 'sharp as a needle,' but rather an old story. Try and 'scare up' some illustration novel and new, like the book ; something startling ; something to be felt, and easily remembered. But don't put it on too thick, overdo the thing, and thus spoil it. 'Let your moderation be known to all men.' Something like the following, will answer all purposes. Try to find a better book, eh ! you might just as well undertake to throw back the waters of a mighty cataract, with a pitch-fork ; climb to heaven on a honey-locust, feet foremost ; dam up the Mississippi with a thimble full of sand ; empty the ocean with a teaspoon ; capsize the Andes, or the Rocky mountains, with a knitting needle, or raise a mighty tornado with a fanning mill. (Stop a minute and take breath.) Yes, you might just as well undertake to scale up the Falls of the Niagara in a potash kettle, with a crow-bar, quench the fires of Ætna with a single dew-drop, or blow out the sun with a hand-bellows—as to look for a nicer, or more interesting book, for yourself and your sons (family included), than the Judge's new and pretty book. And that, as the lawyers would say, is making out a pretty strong case. Nevertheless, for the spice of the thing, you might venture to go one little round more. Yes, indeed, you might just as well undertake to 'jump Jim Crow' in a tar-bucket, or gather up a bushel of fleas, turned loose in a stubble patch; and if that don't do you, just give it up, and welcome.

Seriously, if you think my little book worthy of patronage, speak a good word for it, and that will help the thing along. I do not expect you to like everything in it. It was not written for one only, but for many. I intended to write such a book as the world never saw. And all my readers, I think, will say, that I have done it quite handsomely. Finally, don't do me the injustice to say, that it is a fulsome, disgusting, egotistical work, because I say so much about myself and the favorable and even flattering notices, accorded to me; for what, indeed, would my book be worth minus these things. My great object has been to show that from great obscurity, I had attained an honorable distinction among the great and the good men of earth. And I do know, that I have so written for the encouragement of others, and

for that, purely and solely.   I am not a vain man, I put
on no airs, I cut no swells, and never did, in the palmiest days of my life.   I feel that at best, I am a poor,
frail, erring mortal, and that it is altogether 'by the
grace of God, that I am what I am.'   And if I am
ever so happy as to 'gain a mansion in the skies' as
I confidently anticipate, and that right soon, too,
even there I shall be none other than 'a sinner
saved by grace.'

> 'Tis all my hope, 'tis all my plea,
> For me, the Saviour died for me.'

And blessed be his holy name, now and evermore,
Amen.

PUBLIC MEETING.

Having a little space yet unoccupied, I hasten to fill it with the following proceeding, because my numerous friends have so often and so pressingly desired it. And here it is for them:

Shortly after my late most extraordinary and novel wedding, some of my new neighbor friends convened at the school-house, and by general consent adopted the following preamble and resolution, to wit:

Whereas, the late marriage of Rev. Judge Cotton, long a citizen of Indiana, and the very amiable Miss Jane M. Hamilton, at the bride's own beautiful residence, was a most interesting affair, and as we think utterly too good to be lost, as furnishing an item of interest to the common journals of the county, therefore

Resolved, That a full report of the same be furnished to the Portland City journals for publication, and that the journals of Maine and Indiana, at least, be requested to copy, &c. And here follows the

ORCHARD GROVE WEDDING.

REPORT.

The late wedding of Rev. Judge Cotton, long a citizen of the West, and the amiable Miss Jane Hamilton, at the bride's own beautiful cottage residence, Yarmouth Foreside, Me., Sept. 20th, 1871, was a most romantic and magnificent affair.

Five eminent ministers took part in the pleasing ceremonies, and more than 500 invited and volunteer guests were in attendance on the most pleasing and interesting occasion. Two rows of thrifty, bearing apple trees, belonging to the beautiful premises, were pruned into a perfect and most beautiful arch, or avenue, all richly carpeted with verdant green; and under the direction of Capt. Monroe Buckman, marshal of the day, the vast multitude formed lines opposite to each other, facing inward, down the said two rows of pruned trees, closing together at a proper distance, thus forming an open, oval circle, four or five deep, the shortest in front, presenting a perfect amphitheatre of human faces, one above another, as 'Alps on Alps arise.' At the open end of the oblong, half circle, was a low platform, finely carpeted, for the reception of the happy bride and groom, and their attendants, at the proper time. Just in front of the stand, inside of the ring, were seated the five officiating clergymen, and in the rear of them, sat a beautiful choir of fine and well trained singers. All things being put in a state of readiness, under the direction of the marshal, the happy pair and their attendants were conducted to the stand, Hon. Ammi Mitchell and his most amiable and beau-

tiful lady, being their attendants. A most felicitous
selection indeed. It could not have been better.
When the parties made their appearance on the bal-
cony, the choir, under the leadership of Dr. Burbank,
an eminent practitioner, and one of the finest choris-
ters in the State, struck up a beautiful air and ode,
under the inspiration of which, the parties came
forward to the stand ; heads uncovered, save that
the modest temples of the blushing bride, were
adorned with an evergreen wreath bedecked with
modest flowers. Both were neatly and appropriate-
ly dressed, in a bran-new suit. 'Cap-a-pie.' Not a
leaf fluttered in the breeze, the sun veiling himself
in a cloud, much to the comfort and convenience of
all present. Many of the matrons and maids were
sporting magnificently, beautiful bouquets, to be presented to the Judge at the proper time. What a
scene for a painter ! Many and bitter are the re-
grets, that one was not present on the occasion. At
the close of the ode, the marriage ceremonies were
formally introduced, by Rev. James S. Rice, of
North Pownal, who was assisted therein, by his right
and left hand supporters, thus, Rev. Mr. Sanborn,
of Falmouth, propounded the ordinary marriage vows
to the happy, smiling groom, who stood up firmly
and erect, and in a full, clear voice, responded thus,
to the very agreeable surprise of all present :

'Not intending to deny myself the luxury of inno-

cent freedom and familiarities with my lady friends,
I answer, that the marriage vows which you, Sir,
have just propounded to my consideration, I now
most cheerfully and heartily assume, without any
mental reservation, whatever. And I now say to
you, Sir, and to her, who, in the wonderful, special,
and kind providence of God, is soon, very soon, to become my lawfully wedded, my beloved wife, and I
say it, in the presence of God, and all these witnesses,
that these solemn vows shall at home and abroad,
by me, be carefully, scrupulously and religiously observed and kept; not because I must, but because
'I will' most cheerfully.' Which drew forth a few
hearty Amens, and a general murmur of approving
delight from all present. The Rev. Mr. Fairbanks,
of Cape Elizabeth, now obligated the fair, blushing
bride, who in turn fairly electrified the entire assembly, by her quaint answer, in a full, open voice,
'Sir, reciprocating the vows of my plighted husband,
I answer, I will.' Beautiful, O, how beautiful!

Rev. Mr. Rice, now pronounced the happy pair,
husband and wife, together, in the name of the
Father, Son, and Holy Ghost. And right here, in
a most graceful and dignified manner, the Judge
saluted his bride, in the presence of all the people,
much to their seeming pleasure and amusement.
And it was thought, that the blushing bride recip-

9*

rocated the compliment, quite.as handsomely as she did the marriage vows.

After this little pleasing episode, Rev. Mr. Abbott, Congregational minister, at Yarmouth, offered up a most appropriate and beautiful prayer, earnest, comprehensive and eloquent; every way worthy of the eminent minister who uttered it, and the very pleasing and interesting occasion which called it forth.

Rev. Mr. Hoyt, of 'Chebeague Island,' pronounced the benediction, in an easy, graceful and most imposing manner. Indeed, it would seem that all the officiating clergymen vied with each other to do their very best, in the premises. And the result throughout, was a perfectly finished and polished performance. The choir now sung a beautiful anthem, which enchained the vast assembly, in rapturous delight. The Dr.'s very amiable and accomplished sister, Miss Esther, sung most interestingly; her clear, sweet voice, rang out most distinctly and harmoniously, to the admiration and praise of all present. At the close of this most beautiful performance, the presentation of bouquets, personal congratulation, and friendly greetings, became the general order of the day. And a merry time we had of it, all the way round. Well did the City editors say, 'it was a most novel and imposing affair. And the occasion was made one of a general jollification.' When the excitement had a little abated, the Judge made a few

well-timed and appropriate remarks, thanking all for
their kind attentions, and their beautiful performance,
adding, this is one of the sunniest, happiest days of
my long and eventful life. But think not my friends,
that in the midst of these general joys and hilarities,
that I forget or underrate the dear, sainted wife of
my youth. No, never; nevertheless, but for these
chastening and ever to be cherished remembrances,
I should be almost too happy to live, and for aught I
know I shall yet expire in a thrill of rapturous bliss.
Movements now indicated a general dispersion, when
a lady calling on the judge for one of his pretty puns
on his own marriage, brought all to perfect order
again. To that fair call the judge responded thus:
' That is a very hard request, my friends; if there is
any poetry in Cotton, or any word in the English
language that perfectly rhymes with it, I do not at
this moment apprehend them. I have been thinking
about this matter, and the very best pun that I can
'grind out ' is something like the following:

'It takes a pretty name, my friends, to make a rich and
  pretty pun,
A pun upon my humble name, would only make you
  'lots of fun;'
The groom my worthy bride has gotten,
Is just 'a lot' of Northern Cotton.
  (Loud laughter.)
Well hymen, well, now you have done it,
Else there is no truth in my little sonnet:

And never shall it be forgotten,
You've changed my lovely bride, all into 'COTTON.'
 (Prolonged cheering.)

The next point of attraction, was the dinner table, which was tastefully adorned with wreaths and vases of sweet blushing flowers, and perfectly teeming with the choices viands, done up to order. It was set in the dining hall, and would accommodate 30 or 40 to one sitting, or rather to one standing. Good old Father Groves, the honored Patriarch of Cousin's Island, and his excellent lady, occupied honorary seats at the head of the table, a handsome, well-deserved compliment. After the first table full had been well served, the happy pair repaired to their spacious and beautiful sitting room, followed by their delighted guests, who again congratulated them, and made a general survey of the beautiful cottage premises, and so on, until all had feasted to the full, and were perfectly content. Explanatory of this vast wedding party, and these ample provisions for the occasion, it might be well to say just here, that the wedding would have been a large and magnificent affair, any-how, which suggested the beautiful orchard grove, as the most suitable place for its celebration. And when it became noised abroad, that such was the arrangement, outsiders called upon the parties, to see if they were willing that the entire community should change it from a private, to a picnic wedding, to make it a magnificent ovation, or rather, a grand reception party, as everybody desired to be present on the novel occasion. Certainly not; the more, the better, under such an arrangement. The report took wing, and from City and town, from hill-top and vale, from 'the Islands of the sea,' and from all along the shore, the people came pouring in by scores, with 'baskets and boxes,' crammed chuck full of goodies for the occasion, done up in the very best and latest style of modern housewifery.

The Judge being very highly appreciated as a man, and as a minister, the bride, being a general favorite in the community from her youth up, the number and respectability of the bridal relations, together with the novelty and romance, are the keys that unlock it all. Certainly, such a magnificent marriage was never before celebrated in the State, or hardly anywhere else. And the parties enjoyed it hugely, you may be well assured. It was purely 'a cold water party.' All passed off pleasantly, without a jarring note of discord, to mar the beauty and pleasures of the occasion. Well may it be said, 'it was never so seen in Israel,' or anywhere else.

After the delighted guests had mostly dispersed, the happy pair with a goodly number of their friends, repaired to the landing, on the sea shore, a short half mile distant, where Capt. Jacob Groves was in waiting with his fine sailing craft, Cornelia; and a pleasant sail out upon the bay, closed the pleasing occurrences of the day. But late in the evening, after the happy bride and groom had retired to rest, a very large and most civil serenading party struck up one of the most sweet and mellow airs of the season, immediately under the bridal chamber window. And the parties say, that the music was most bewitchingly sweet and fascinating. After enjoying the intellectual luxury, for a season in quiet, the delighted pair appeared at the window, where they were vociferously and loudly congratulated. The Judge made them a short speech, thanked them all very kindly, for their finely executed compliment, and their soul-stirring music; then, bidding them a most warm and hearty good-night, closed the window and retired, under the moving inspiration of three long, loud and animating cheers, from the happy band of skillful serenaders. And thus closed the varied and pleasing sayings and doings of Judge Cotton's second wedding. That he may long live to enjoy the very agreeable society of his most amiable, most intelligent and most pious lady; and the comforts of his new and beautiful home, is the general wish and prayer of all. Amen.

THE REPORTER.

Yarmouth, Me., Oct. 1st, 1871.

Note by the Judge, 1872.

This second wedding of mine, as might reasonably be supposed from the above graphic and glowing report, produced quite a general excitement in the literary and religious circles of the county. All the Portland City editors really 'puffed' it abroad. The Boston *Herald* quoted it, sure. And I am informed that the Lewiston *Journal*, and the New York *Tribune* and other journals passed it around. A friend just returned from an European voyage, said, it met his eyes in Edinburgh, Scotland, and then again at Liverpool, England. Another friend says, that it met him in Nebraska, and that it was known all over California, in less than a month after its celebration. It has gone out into all the world, to the very ends of the earth, I reckon. Was ever the like before? That I should have such a magnificent wedding, and win such a pretty home, such a superior wife, and such a flattering world-wide notoriety, in the kind providence of God, fills my heart with gratitude and praise to God ; and with honest pride and heart-felt gratitude, I conclude this report.

This very magnificent and romantic wedding would not have been accorded to me, had I spent all of my spare dimes for 'rum and tobacco,' and all my leisure hours in loafing around.

And then when I trip over my fine carpets, up
stairs and down, loll about in my easy chairs, my
lounges, my sofas, and my beautiful vine arbor, when
I sport my pretty, gold watch-chain and gold specta-
cles, presented to me by my superior, good lady, when
I survey my very pretty, five acre lot, my thrifty,
fruitful orchard, and my model garden, when I look
out upon the beautiful Bay and Islands, and my
beautiful surroundings generally, I am tempted to
ask myself, 'am I in a trance, in the dream land,'
or am I still an inhabitant of earth, if so, as other-
where expressed, then indeed have I neither served
the church, nor the country in vain. My donation
of $500.00 to Moore's Hill College, was the enter-
ing wedge to all this good fortune ; explanation hereafter. What saith it ? 'Give and it shall be given
to you, good measure, pressed down and running
over.' And if that is not literally being fulfilled in
me, I should very much like to know what would
be. 'Surely goodness and mercy has followed me
all the days of my life.' And I may well say with
the poet :—

> My cup of blessings overflows,
> And joy exalts my heart.

O, I am almost too happy to live, and do not expect to live long. The will of God be done. Amen
and amen.

I have very many choice poems still on hand, but I cannot quote them here. My book will be too large anyhow, for a sketch-book, but I will venture to insert just one more, which I appreciate very highly, and is applicable in all coming time. And this is it. A Presidential campaign ode, which I 'ground out ' for 1860, and pronounced at a Republican mass meeting, to the manifest delight of the vast assemblage.

THE SHIP OF STATE.

Our gallant ship of State, now standing out to sea,
Is sound in all her timbers, and from objections free;
'Though tempest-tossed and driven, as oft she 's been
    before,
She 'll ride the surging billows, and safely reach the shore.
With Lincoln at the helm, and Hamlin at his side,
Our gallant ship of State, will every storm outride.

That men should widely disagree, in freedom 's land
    along,
Is right and reasonable to suppose, as saith my humble
    song;
But never dare abuse those rights, nor 'tremble in the
    knees, '
Then think and speak and write and vote, precisely as
    you please,
    With Lincoln at the helm, &c.

I love an honest Democrat, I love him good and hearty,
But in my soul do I despise, false men of our own party.
O for strong nerves, for sound back-bone, in men of rank
       and station,
Such are the men to love in song, and such to rule the
       nation.
     With Lincoln at the helm, &c.

'Tis cheering to the heart to know there is a power above,
That rules the nations of the earth in justice, truth, and
       love ;
And that oppression, sin, and shame are odious in His
       sight,
And all the advocates of wrong He'll surely put to flight.
     With Lincoln at the helm, &c.

The masses of our people are honest to the core,
Convince them they are surely wrong, and they will err
       no more;
Full well I know 'tis hard to do, but still it can be done,
Illume their minds with light and truth, and lo ! the work
       is done.
     With Lincoln at the helm, &c.

Be active freemen, active, while it is called to-day,
And whatever else you may omit, do not forget to pray;
We should acknowledge God the more, as howling tem-
       pests lower,
His name a shield and buckler is, a safeguard and a tower.
     With Lincoln at the helm, &c.

When honest Abe shall man the helm, and put the craft
       in trim,
Thousands who oppose him now, will rally then to him;

The howling tempest cease its roar, which threatened us
    so long,
Then all the world shall feel and see our Union bands are
    strong.
    With Lincoln at the helm, &c.

Let great men flicker as they may, the yeomanry are true,
And 'tis with them, my countrymen, that we have much
    to do;
Upon the honest masses, pour in a flood of light,
And victory will crown the day, and now my friends,
    good-night.

Anything in that unworthy of a minister of Christ?

I have not quoted the entire poem, but the sub-
stance of it. It went off, without pushing, and I
made my mark handsomely. I remodeled it, for
Grant and Colfax, and then again, for Grant and
Wilson. And now, if I could 'grab' a little out of
it, as readily as Grant and Butler did the dimes out
of the Treasury, I should be content. But as Pi-
late said, 'what I have written, I have written,' and
so it must remain. I will now conclude this chapter, with one more of the very flattering public
notices, that have been accorded to me, from time
to time, during my past very honorable and eventful history. I do it, more to encourage the little
boys, and to make out my case, as a lawyer would

say, than to flatter my own vanity; although I feel
very comfortable under the operation, you may well
be assured.   Read it, boys, and then say what you
will do for yourselves!

PRESIDENTIAL ELECTOR.

MR. EDITOR: I notice that several persons are through the columns of your paper, presenting the claims of their friends for nomination at the Union Conventions, and to be up with the fashion of the times, I would respectfully mention the name of our old friend, Rev. Judge A. J. Cotton, in connection with the office of Presidential Elector for this District. The Judge is 'some' on the stump, as well as in the pulpit and on the bench; there are no better Union men living, and I know there are none more willing to work in the cause. As he is getting along in years, and will probably soon retire from the active scenes of this world, it has occurred to me that there could be no more appropriate closing of a well-spent life than registering his vote as a Presidential Elector for President of the United States in favor of some man.

'Pledged but to Truth, to Liberty and Law.'

And certainly no more flattering testimonial of the esteem and confidence in which Judge Cotton is held by his fellow-citizens, could be offered than by tendering him the nomination for the above office. Let us do it.   SOLDIER.

A POEM:

RECITED BY PRESIDENT LINCOLN.

Having a page or two kindly accorded to me, I hasten with pleasure to fill them with that most beautiful poem, about which President Lincoln once said :—

'There is a poem, which has been a great favorite with me for years, which was first shown to me when a young man, by a friend, and which I afterwards saw and cut from a newspaper, and learned by heart. I would, he continued, give a great deal to know who wrote it, but I have never been able to ascertain.'

Here it is, for your pleasurable and profitable entertainment.

'O, WHY SHOULD THE SPIRIT OF MORTAL BE PROUD.'

O why should the spirit of mortal be proud ?
Like a swift, fleeting meteor, a fast-flying cloud,
A flash of the lightning, a break of the wave,
He passeth from life to rest in the grave.

The leaves of the oak and the willow shall fade,
Be scattered around and together be laid,
And the young and the old, and the low and the high,
Shall moulder to dust, and together shall lie.

The infant and mother attended and loved ;
The mother that infant's affection who proved;
The husband that mother and infant who blessed,
Each, all, are away to their dwellings of rest.

The hand of the king that the sceptre hath borne;
·The brow of the priest that the mitre hath worn;
The eye of the sage and the heart of the brave,
Are hidden and lost in the depths of the grave.

The peasant, whose lot was to sow and to reap;
The herdsman, who climbed with his goats up the steep;
The beggar, who wandered in search of his bread,
Have faded away like the grass that we tread.

So the multitude goes, like the flower or the weed,
That withers away to let others succeed;
So the multitude comes, even those we behold,
To repeat every tale that has often been told.

For we are the same as our fathers have been;
We see the same sights that our fathers have seen—
We drink the same stream and we view the same sun,
And run the same course that our fathers have run.

The thoughts we are thinking our fathers would think;
From the death we are shrinking our fathers would shrink;
To the life we are clinging they also would cling;
But it speeds for us all like a bird on the wing.

They loved, **but the story** we cannot unfold;
They scorned, but the heart of the haughty is cold;
They grieved, but no wail from their slumber will come;
They joyed, but the tongue of their gladness is dumb.

They died, aye ! they died; we things that are **now**,
That walk on the turf that lies over their brow,
And make in their dwellings a transient abode,
Meet the things that they met on their pilgrimage road.

Yea ! hope and despondency, pleasure and pain,
We mingle together in sunshine and rain;
And the smile and the tear, the song and the dirge,
Still follow each other, like surge upon surge.

'Tis the wink of an eye, 'tis the draught of a breath,
From the blossom of health to the paleness of death;
From the gilded saloon to the bier and the shroud—
O, why should the spirit of mortal be proud ?

O, indeed ! is that not most beautiful, beautiful ?

JANE HAMILTON COTTON.

Portland, Me., Nov. 5, 1873.